Penguin Books

R. Stonehouse

THE ORCHARD THIEVES

Elizabeth Jolley was born in the industrial Midlands of England in 1923. She moved to Western Australia in 1959 with her husband and three children. She has worked in a variety of occupations and is currently cultivating a small orchard and teaching part time at Curtin University of Technology.

Elizabeth Jolley is acclaimed as one of Australia's leading writers and has received an AO, honorary doctorates from WAIT (now Curtin University) and Macquarie University, and the ASAL Gold Medal for her contribution to Australian literature. Australian literary journals and anthologies have published her fiction and poetry, which, together with her plays, have been broadcast on British and Australian radio.

She has published three collections of short fiction, a collection of short essays, *Central Mischief*, and eleven novels, of which *Mr Scobie's Riddle* and *My Father's Moon* won the *Age* Book of the Year Award, *Milk and Honey* the NSW Premier's Award, *The Well* the Miles Franklin Award, *The Georges' Wife* the National Book Council Banjo Award for fiction, *Cabin Fever* the FAW ANA Literature Award, and *The Sugar Mother* the France-Australia Literary Translation Award.

Also by Elizabeth Jolley

Five Acre Virgin and other stories

The Travelling Entertainer and other stories

Palomino

The Newspaper of Claremont Street

Mr Scobie's Riddle

Woman in a Lampshade

Miss Peabody's Inheritance

Foxybaby

Milk and Honey

The Well

The Sugar Mother

My Father's Moon

Cabin Fever

Central Mischief

The Georges' Wife

THE ORCHARD THIEVES

ELIZABETH JOLLEY

PENGUIN BOOKS

Penguin Books Australia Ltd
487 Maroondah Highway, PO Box 257
Ringwood, Victoria, 3134, Australia
Penguin Books Ltd
Harmondsworth, Middlesex, England
Viking Penguin, A Division of Penguin Books USA Inc.
375 Hudson Street, New York, New York 10014, USA
Penguin Books Canada Limited
10 Alcorn Avenue, Toronto, Ontario, Canada, M4V 3B2
Penguin Books (NZ) Ltd
Cnr Rosedale and Airborne Roads, Albany, Auckland, New Zealand

First published by Viking Australia, 1995
This edition published by Penguin Books Australia Ltd, 1997
1 3 5 7 9 10 8 6 4 2

Typeset in 11/15 Al Prosperal by Midland Typesetters, Maryborough, Victoria.
Made and printed in Australia by Australian Print Group, Maryborough, Victoria.

National Library of Australia
Cataloguing-in-Publication data:

Jolley, Elizabeth, 1923-
The orchard thieves.
ISBN 014 025 211 8
I. Title.
A823.3

For Harry and Hannah Levey.

And for Leonard Jolley

who borrowed the maps from

the Leveys and never returned them.

ACKNOWLEDGEMENTS

I would like to express my thanks to the Curtin University of Technology for the continuing privilege of being with students and colleagues in the School of Communication and Cultural Studies and for the provision of a room in which to write. I would like, in particular, to thank Don Watts, Peter Reeves, Brian Dibble, Barbara Milech, Ian Reid, Anne Brewster and Don Grant. In addition I would like to thank John Maloney, John de Laeter, Don Yeats and Ross Bennett. A special thanks is offered to Nancy McKenzie who, for a great many years, has typed my manuscripts. She is endlessly patient. I would like as well to thank Kay Ronai, an especially thoughtful and sensitive editor. In addition, I would like to thank all those people at Penguin Books Australia who work so hard to produce and market the finished books. In particular I would like to thank Bruce Sims for his encouragement, his wisdom and his kindness.

'Three Miles to One Inch' was originally published in the *New Yorker* in 1994.

PREFACE

'If you have the house,' the middle sister said to the aunt, the eldest sister, 'if you have the house you'll have to pay us each one-third of the current market price. One-third each of the value of the place.'

'That's right,' the youngest sister's husband said, 'this is prime land, this is, a paddock left behind in the middle of a high-class residential suburb *and* practically on the river at that. You'd be living in a most expensive area and you'd have to pay for it. 'Now,' he warmed to his subject, 'if them trees were to be chopped down, the big trees I mean, there'd be river views. There's one or two places around where there's land left wasted. Fetching good prices they are.'

The youngest sister, who seemed to have no opinions, no voice and no personality since her marriage, did not say anything.

The three sisters all had memories of being little girls together in that place, that house in a paddock left in the suburb.

The youngest sister's husband had nothing to remember, he was simply the father of the two grandsons.

'Do you remember,' the middle sister, speaking quickly, asked the eldest sister, the aunt, 'that Christmas when you tried to sell your doll?'

'No,' the eldest sister, the aunt, said. 'No, I don't.'

Part One

THREE MILES TO ONE INCH

'These little Limmes
These Eys and Hands which here I find,
These rosie Cheeks wherwith my Life begins,
Where have ye been? Behind
What Curtain were ye from me hid so long
Where was? in what Abyss, my Speaking Tongue?'

THOMAS TRAHERNE

THE AUNT WANTED to go out by herself. The aunt said she wanted quiet and fresh air. The aunt said she would walk alone. She said the nephews must walk with their grandmother. 'This once,' she said. 'Your grandmother would like a walk,' she told them. 'Go with your grandmother.' The aunt said the nephews could not go with her unless they walked first with their grandmother. The nephews could come with her later, the aunt said, she did not want the grandmother to explore with them along the cliff. The cliff path, the secret path on the rocky cliff, the aunt said, was uneven. The grandmother would not manage the path, she said. All those rocks.

The grandmother thought about the aunt wanting to walk alone. She thought it might be because the aunt wanted to meet someone. She would like, she told the grandsons, to have a walk with them. The grandmother turned the thoughts over in her mind. If the aunt wanted to meet someone all by herself, she, the grandmother, did not know who it could be. She hoped that no harm would come to the aunt. She was afraid that the aunt might be hurt in some way.

The grandsons told the grandmother that they did not want to walk. They did not want to walk anywhere. Because of this, the walk, as it turned out, was something of an ordeal for the grandmother. The grandsons started straight away to race ahead, disappearing in the gardens all along the road. They disappeared for such a long time that the grandmother thought they must be lost or that they might have turned back and gone home.

The grandsons, reappearing as if from nowhere, climbed like monkeys into the street trees and, with strange inhuman noises, burrowed into the woody hibiscus and oleander bushes. The grandmother feared hidden broken glass and thought of their bare fragile feet.

The grandmother called the grandsons to come out from the bushes. The grandsons, obeying, walked immediately behind the grandmother almost treading on her heels. The grandmother turned, smiling, and told the grandsons to look yonder at the lemon tree there in the deep green of someone's back garden. She admired, for them, white roses and a variety of hibiscus, apricot coloured, the flowers, she said, as big as dinner plates. 'Look you,' she said to the grandsons, 'at that pretty house and the pretty fence.' A white fence, she told them, is nice with geraniums climbing over the pickets.

Crappy house. That's a crappy house, the grandsons told each other, and a crappy fence, they said. Crappy crap. Another crappy house. The grandsons counted the crappy houses, one after the other. Crap, one grandson said. Crap, the other replied. It was all crap, they agreed. Yeah. The grandsons disappeared once more.

In the corner shop the grandmother said that the grandsons could choose a chocolate bar each. The grandmother told the grandsons that the coin-operated game would not work without money. She told them to leave the knobs and handles alone. As the grandsons unwrapped their chocolate, the grandmother noticed suddenly how small their hands were still. She hoped, as they all three walked slowly home, that the aunt would not wait and wait on the cliff path for someone who, promising to come there, would not come.

When it was time to do the shopping at the supermarket, neither of the grandsons wanted to go with the grandmother. First one, then the other, said they would wait at home for the aunt. They would be perfectly all right by themselves, they said.

During previous visits the grandsons had made a dash for the shopping trolleys, one each, which they took with their own engine noises and remarkably realistic squealing brakes down the first aisle and round the corner and back up the next aisle and down the third, while the grandmother was still studying her shopping list. She told the first grandson, as he rushed by, soap powder. She moved quickly out of his way as he put himself in reverse. She told the second grandson detergent and floor polish, but he was already too far away in bread, cakes, biscuits, rolls and muffins.

The supermarket resounded with their engines as they changed from first gear to second and up to third somewhere inside their thin narrow chests.

It could be, the grandmother thought, as she prowled in the strangely quiet supermarket, that she might go, on one of these days stretching out into evenings, when the aunt went out alone, to the path along the river. It was possible that she might see someone and, from a little distance of course, sum him or her up at once.

'It's vascular,' the doctor said, when the grandmother tried to explain that the noise in her head was like a pump going. He went on to say that he'd had head noises himself for years. Everyone had noises in their heads. 'Bells,' he said, 'and not bicycle or church.' Everyone had noises in their heads, himself included. Not like mine, the grandmother told him. Sometimes, she said, she was embarrassed that people might be listening to her head and what was going on in there.

While the doctor wrote a prescription for her the grandmother thought about the long grass in her orchard and the way in which this dry bleached grass pursued her, as if on fire already, whenever she made her way up the slope. She thought of the plums, the Satsuma, the golden drop and blue prune plums. They would be ready for picking. The prune plums in particular never failed to surprise her, they were like something in a fairy-tale illustration, an intense blue, hanging secretly in the deep green of the leaves. The bloom on these small vividly coloured fruits gave an impression of a delicate mist hovering about the trees. She often picked some plums early and put them along the kitchen window-sill to ripen. Forgetting them, she was agreeably surprised to see them whenever she went into the kitchen.

Some mornings, like this morning early, the grandmother would study an old road atlas, three miles to one inch, only certain pages of course, as she was familiar only with two or three small areas in Great Britain. She put on her reading glasses and, as well, held the magnifying glass over the maps.

This morning she could not seem to find

Sparkbrook. She had the Stratford Road, all right, out of Birmingham. Farm Road, there was no farm, went off Stratford Road. Sparkbrook was marked, she was sure, but perhaps where one map joined another. She knew the Stratford Road through Henley-in-Arden to Stratford. Once she had ridden a bicycle all the way to the edge of the Cotswolds where her boarding school was. The way went through Henley-in-Arden, through Stratford-on-Avon, there it all was clearly on the map, through Shipston-on-Stour, on to Upper Brailes and Lower Brailes and on to the three villages of Sibford Ferris, Sibford Gower and Burdrop. The names and the recollections were a kind of poem. At the end of that term, her last, she rode all the way back on the bicycle, the sixty-seven miles to Solihull, the place her own grandmother moved to when she left Sparkbrook.

The grandmother, waking too early before it was light, and before the birds, was overwhelmed with dismal thoughts. There was the family visit and the shoutings of the grandson's father the day before, and an unexpected reproach and criticism spoken during an early birthday telephone call for the aunt from the middle sister living on the other side of the world. (The aunt had refused to come to the telephone.) But worse was the anxious expression in the gentle eyes of the elder grandson and the indecision shown by her younger daughter, the grandson's mother, in the face of their father's loud angry voice. And then there was her own stupid and unforgivable forgetfulness about small but important items, the wholemeal bread for one thing. *That bread.* The aunt said, what did *bread* matter for heaven's sake and, she said, she, the grandmother should *not* have answered the phone at lunch-time when the whole family was milling around in the kitchen. The aunt went out for the rest of the day by herself.

The nephews piled all the nicest things they could find in the house in the doorway of the aunt's room.

As the light crept up the sky outside her window the grandmother heard the first soft chirpings of the birds, tentative bird voices, scarcely a song, little bird whisperings as one, then another, made the first bird sounds. It was like hearing the grandchildren waking up and beginning to talk to each other in the room across the passage, the way her own children, the three sisters had, years ago, played small quiet games together at daybreak.

The grandmother has never forgotten the way in which the aunt, waiting her turn, took and held first one newly born nephew and then the second nephew when he was newly born. It seemed to the grandmother then that the aunt, straight away, held each new baby, in turn, somehow as if in the palms of her large hands. It was as if the lineaments for both children's distinctive and separate features were carved, in advance, for their expected coming on these capable and empty hands. It was as if the stick-like little thighs and arms fattened and dimpled visibly in the caress, shaped by the way in which the aunt cupped her hands to receive them both, first one and then the other. The aunt's love for her nephews, the grandmother thought then, lit up her plain face and softened, with a previously hidden tenderness, her angular body. Whenever the nephews came to visit, the aunt made them hers, in her looking at them, in her sitting and walking with them, in their going to bed and in their getting up. Her voice, which was deep, became deeper and softer when she spoke or read to them. The nephews, right from the beginning, every time they came, came into the aunt's world. The grandmother knew it was because of the aunt they were still willing, now that they were no longer tiny children, to come. She did not mind at all and took pleasure in their visits and the wrecking of the ordinary childless tidiness in her home. It was decided that the grandsons should stay (they called it sleeping over) because of it being the aunt's birthday the next day even though the aunt declared she had no birthdays now.

The journey to school on the three-miles-to-one-inch map held many pleasures. For one thing, the grandmother liked her school uniform very much. She liked it so much that she never liked to dress up in her red jumper and skirt on changing days (Wednesday and Saturday afternoons after games). The school uniform was a green tunic with a square neck, it was loose with three box pleats, front and back, and gathered at the waist by a woven sort of belt called a girdle, also green. The tunic was worn over a cream-coloured blouse, with a school tie, or, in winter, over a dark-green jumper, with the school colours of brown and gold showing at the neck and the wrists. Later she became very fond of her nurse's uniform.

Sometimes she wondered why she preferred uniform. Perhaps she thought, now, that it simplified life, giving the wearer a plain but recognized status - if that was what was needed. It also meant that a person did not stand out to be criticised or laughed at because of an odd choice in clothes. The uniform, she knew now, made for the safe and the ordinary. A long time ago before all this, the grandmother recalled, someone's mother passed on a navy-blue tunic which was too big for her. Long before she was old enough for school, she dressed up in it, bunching it up in front with the girdle and, going in to where her father sat at his desk, she told him that if anyone came calling for her he was to tell them she had left and gone away to school . . .

When the very young mother of the new grandson, the first born, cried because breastfeeding presented a problem, the grandmother sat on the side of the young mother's bed and, with authority, pressed the grandson's head and his anger towards the engorged breast. The grandmother felt competent in her clean cotton frock, especially as the grandson's regular swallowing was, at once, the only sound in the room. The young mother forgot her tears and laughed, saying that, because of the crisp blue stuff of the grandmother's sleeves, it was like having a real nurse at home looking after her.

Perhaps, the grandmother thought, as she put away the three-miles-to-one-inch maps, that she should consider these days now, these times, these early mornings as being the happiest in her life, since there was no way of knowing what lay ahead. She tried to remember where she had left her gardening gloves. She would make a point of pulling up weeds for ten minutes every day. She had, she knew, great strength and determination in her fingers. With this last thought she remembered once more the power of the pretend uniform and the small, relaxed, but subdued laughter both she and her youngest daughter, the grandson's mother, allowed themselves in the presence of the hungry baby. Pushing the remnants of discord and unhappiness from her mind, she looked forward instead to the afternoon when she would drag the tenacious grass out from the lavender and possibly sweep up a wine box full of fallen leaves and tip them in the rose bed with the hope of enriching the worn-out earth.

Sometimes during the afternoons there was something about the changing light as the sun moved across over the trees, which made the grandmother forget how many years had gone by. She would find herself expecting her own three daughters to come home from their respective schools and immediately begin trying on each other's clothes or, borrowing from each other, pens and books and earrings and hats ... calling out, all the time, teasing remarks and items of schoolgirl gossip.

Sometimes, just after putting away the precious inches of the road atlas, perhaps because of no longer being in the places marked there, the grandmother dropped things; a knife clattered in the metal sink or a bowl chipped and cracked on the tap. The quickness of thought, she told herself then, is too quick for the body. It was surprising that she should remember so much when she was very forgetful. She wondered why this was.

It was the Stratford Road, out from Birmingham to Sparkbrook, which brought the grandmother's own grandfather's voice, the sound of his voice and his head coming, grizzled, round the door of the room where she and her sister sat. They sat playing together on the carpet, in front of the fire, with the Christmas dolls and all the little piles of folded dolls' clothes. Did they know, their grandfather wanted to ask, how many little girls, like themselves, were either kidnapped or run over and killed on the Stratford Road, just down there where Farm Road went off Stratford Road, just a little way down from where they, their grandfather and grandmother, lived.

A kidnapping, her own grandfather said then, was as bad as a road accident because, he explained, children belonged to their parents and grandparents right from before they were born. And they were cherished. Did they, the two of them, there on that carpet, understand just how much they were cherished? Cherished, he said, and brought up with nothing spared and then, in a flash, taken away suddenly. Kidnap and sudden death in an accident were, he said, as if the earth itself had cracked open, revealing a black bottomless cave into which the child just disappeared for ever, leaving broken hearts to make do and mend the best way they could. Broken hearts, broken like this, he said, never do mend, not properly. Kidnap and road accidents were not the only way children disappeared, he said, not at all the only way they disappeared.

The grandmother, in her own reading later, much

later, fitted fairy story and legend and real life together. It seemed to her that legends were attempts to explain happenings which were too painful and hard for human endurance. She wanted to explain something of this to the grandsons. One day, on a rug on the lawn, the grandmother read aloud to the grandsons. She held them both by an ankle, one hand to one ankle on each grandson. She sat with the book in her lap. She was, she told them, going to read them the story of Proserpina and the pomegranate seeds and how the little girl, Proserpina, disobeying her mother, disappeared one bright sunny day while playing on the seashore. The story, the grandmother explained, described the way in which Proserpina's mother, Ceres, was heartbroken. She searched all over the world, asking everyone she met, had they seen her little girl, her most precious possession. The grandmother explained that Proserpina was also known as Persephone and that her mother, then, was called Demeter. It was important, she said, to be correct with the names. Ceres or Demeter, she said, was the goddess of the corn, of the harvest. The grandmother told the grandsons to listen to the part of the story which described how Ceres, during her search, stops at a castle to look after a baby prince who is unable to thrive. She read to the grandsons:

> Ceres sat before the hearth with the child in her lap, the fire-light making her shadow dance upon the ceiling overhead. She undressed the little prince and bathed him all over with some fragrant liquid out of a vase . . .

The grandmother paused to explain that the baby laughed and clapped his little hands and then:

> Ceres suddenly laid him, all naked as he was, in the hollow among the red-hot embers. She then raked the ashes over him and turned quietly away . . .

When the prince's mother saw this, the grandmother said, she was very upset and grabbed her baby out of the hot coals. Ceres was scornful and asked the mother if she imagined that children could become immortal if they were not tempered in the greatest heat of the fire.

It was during this part of the story that the grandsons simply slipped from the grandmother's grasp and disappeared with a slight rustling of dry leaves into the surrounding bushes.

Alone on the grey rug, in the deeply shaded garden, the grandmother began to understand that it was not until she was a grandmother herself that she, because of her own love for her grandsons, realized how much she, as a small child, had been loved.

And the pity was that it was too late to acknowledge this to anyone. It was no longer possible to offer, unsolicited, a kiss, a caress or a tender phrase backwards, as it were, over her shoulder. Recalling momentarily the pain of the telephone reprimand, well deserved she was sure, and only one of many, the grandmother came to a very real truth, which was that the great love which holds the mother to the child does not necessarily travel in the other direction, from the child to the mother. She understood also that she would not be the only person in the world to have discovered this. She had, at times during her life, found herself offering thanks even to the cross old man, her own grandfather, in small silent words, scarcely moving her lips, but still with fervour as if saying a prayer.

Ancient legends, she said to herself on the rug, come from real and unbearable grief. She thought she would write to the grandsons and equip them with this truth. She would include the inescapable suffering of bereavement, of rejection, of jealousy and of remorse. The grandsons, she was sure, would read in time the great writings which included all these. In the meantime they would have her letters. Children, even when they would not listen, would, out of curiosity, gobble up written words. Children were naturally curious.

The grandmother, reassured by the noise, the steady beating as of a piston and a cylinder in her head, folded up the rug and went indoors. Sometimes it was as if a valve, or something like that, was permanently open, stuck, so that there was, in her head, a steady pouring as of an ancient pump, well into its stride and the water flowing without effort. She did not mind this either. It was, in a sense, reassuring that there was something sustained and continuing. Mostly she had other things to think about, like the aunt for example. The eldest daughter was tall, too tall, tall enough to weep, at one time, about being too tall. She walked with long steps, like a man, mannish, the grandmother thought, but kindly remembering the boyish little girl. Mannish, she thought now, and it was never spoken. The aunt was the manager. She had all the keys in a bunch of her own. The grandmother never minded. There had never been any thought or possibility of a marriage. In the world inhabited by the aunt, the men were either married or they were men who preferred the company and the affection of other men or else, covertly, they were both. There were, as well, those men who chose women on whose reputation, social standing and income they could depend. They, these men, described themselves as being in special occupations as consultants in management, in real estate, in fashion and in food. They were agents selling, on secret commission, other people's products. They wrote up wine and restaurants and the elegant homes of the affluent in lyrical but repetitive language. Sham, but believing in themselves, what else could they do. The grandmother thought about the thick hedges of coarse bleached hair and the slack lips. She had noticed the quick sidelong glances of deception in the presence of wives innocent of certain business dealings. She understood that there was place enough for all this and perhaps more besides. The important thing, she thought, was recognition and acceptance that they were not for the aunt.

Even when the youngest daughter was writing out her wedding invitations the aunt (who was not an aunt then) wept silently, admitting in her desperation that, as the eldest, she should have been the first to be married. Even as she was saying this she said she knew the idea was an ancient one from fairy tales and romantic novels and she laughed while she was crying. Whenever the grandmother thought about this, it was not hard for her to remember the tears trembling along the aunt's eyelashes.

The grandmother thought of the aunt wanting, as she said, to walk alone. The grandmother imagined the aunt sitting high up where the river bank was cliff. She would be sitting there watching the changing colour of the water as the day moved slowly through the afternoon towards the evening. The river there was wide. From one hour to the next there could be, on its surface, an ice-blue calm changing to a greenish blue and, a little later, to a sea-green metallic sheet and, almost at once, the water would be as if whipped up into waves with frothy white crests, an animation threatening a storm. Later, still, the waves would settle once more, this time into a slate-purple peacefulness, matching the evening sky at sunset.

This river had been ever a reminder to the grandmother and the aunt that they and the two younger sisters had travelled. This place, with all the differences, and the river was one of these, had become their home. The three miles to one inch was an atlas of roads in the other place, the major roads in red and the minor in blue. The forests, the hills, the mountains, the cities, the towns and even the smallest villages - everything connected by roads could be found. And the English rivers, the Cam, the Thames, the Wey and the Severn, these in particular from the grandmother's experience and memory, were little if in comparison, making this river look, in places, like a wide blue lake. Sometimes, even from the clean sand of this river, it was possible to catch a moment of the special fragrance of those other rivers, a reminder of the brown water between narrow, grass-covered banks, often mud trodden by cows being herded for milking, and overhung with willow trees, their thin branches and leaves trailing over and in the water.

The grandmother knew that the grandsons came to visit because of the aunt. She understood too that it was a possibility that the aunt, by walking alone, by insisting on taking a walk alone on that high-up place (and she really did walk alone, for who was there of any worth to match the aunt?), was giving the nephews to the grandmother for the whole afternoon.

The grandmother understood too, without being told, that the aunt would not, if there was someone, if she was seeing someone, bring him or her home in case it never came to anything. The aunt was shy. She was shy and gentle, both qualities demanded privacy.

The grandmother told the grandsons that it was high time that the aunt should come home. She told them that they would go together to look for the aunt. They would stalk the aunt if stalking became necessary. They must follow her tracks and catch her. They, the grandsons must show her, the grandmother, the secret paths along the river. She would, she said, manage the rocks. For wasn't it she, herself, who had taken the aunt for walks there, once upon a time, long ago. It was important she told the grandsons that they find the aunt. They must hurry, she told them, as they set off at dusk. The grandmother hoped that the river paths, unlike the roads and houses in the suburb and the trolleys in the supermarket, were not crap. She hoped they were not crappy crap. She hoped that the aunt's game and the secret paths, the rocks and the rock pools along the river beaches would remain uncrapped for as long as possible.

Little lights were beginning to appear along the far bank as the grandmother and the grandsons followed a single pathway about the width of a man's boot. It reminded the grandmother of the path made by a small flock of geese as they followed the gander. Five geese to a gander, a hand of geese, the grandmother remembered, walking one behind the other through the grass. The path was the width of the aunt's shoe, one foot being placed, in the manner of geese, directly in front of the other as she walked. Small half moons of trodden grass on either side suggested the thin nimble feet of the grandsons running and leaping, repeatedly following and leading the aunt.

A flock of black cockatoos, showing white flashes in their wings, flew screaming, breasting the purple-brown river. The black cloud of marauding birds seemed suddenly to dip into the water and, rising with fresh screams, they turned and flew in the other direction.

The sweet yet sharp fragrance of the warm

evening reminded the grandmother of her own small orchard and the pleasure of walking there on summer nights. The air, rising cool and damp from the river, picked up the scent of the dry grass and the dry leaves and the few late flowers remaining after the hot summer. Because water is the last thing to get dark the river was too pale and made a poor background for the path the fast-rising moon tried to provide. The grandsons, running like little dogs to and fro and in circles, made one of their disappearances, sliding with hardly any sound down an old watercourse. The grandmother, remembering, thought of their torn and sand-stained clothes. In the following silence she heard the river water whispering along the foot of the small cliff and, from the surrounding grass, there was a thin, persistent, monotonous music from the grasshoppers and other insects. The grandmother told herself that she should have taken this walk earlier. She should have, on one of the afternoons stretching into the evenings, walked out to where the aunt would be and there she, the grandmother, might have seen someone and known, in one glimpse, whether he or she was worthy or unworthy of the aunt.

Once, long ago, when playing on the grass-covered pit mounds of her childhood, the grandmother had come near to a sinister and forbidden place, an old pit shaft fenced with single wires attached to rotted and leaning posts. The coarse-tufted grass grew up to and over the edges of the shaft so that it was not possible to guess the true edges. It was not possible either to know how deep the shaft was and it was a surprise to discover the horror that it was not deep at all, but filled in almost to the top and furnished with all the ugliness of displaced human existence. An old sofa lay there on its side, the flock and springs bursting, as if through infected wounds in the discoloured cloth, as if someone, hiding, was living there and would return at nightfall to this remnant of ordinary household, hideous in the desolate place.

The grandmother, catching sight briefly of the grandsons ahead of her in the fast-falling dusk, called out to them to keep away from fenced-off hollows along the river, places where sand and rocks had been quarried and where water collected, out of sight, and you could never know, her voice cracked as she called to them, you could never know how deep that water might be; and you could never know what or who might be lurking in the castor-oil bushes, thriving as they do in deserted places, like stinging nettles, encroaching, in the wake of human habitation and human use of the land. They were approaching just such a place, and the grandmother, recalling that there had been a derelict house there at one time, felt suddenly afraid. The grandsons had disappeared as if gone for ever. It was almost too dark to make out the path. The rocks were troublesome underfoot and her voice had lost all power. Her skirts caught in the woody stems of ancient bushes; aromatic, red currant and rosemary, she thought, as she stumbled down into the damp and overgrown hollow. She, fearful of hidden, jagged corrugated iron, coils of old wire, old timber with rusty nails protruding, thought suddenly of snakes. All at once she was seized upon on both sides, her clothes clutched by thin fingers and the clutching was accompanied by the familiar small rustlings which seemed, from the start, to be characteristic of any movements made by the grandsons. They, one on each side of the grandmother, seemed to be hauling her upwards as stones and loose gravel gave way beneath her feet. The grandmother, even as she was dragged upwards, wondered at the strength of the grandsons knowing, as she did, how slender and vulnerable their little boyish bodies were beneath her apparently merciless scrubbings every night when she bathed them; little frogs, she thought then, as they slid from her soaped cloth and disappeared under the warm water.

Just as quickly as they appeared, the grandsons disappeared once more into a deep, dry corrugation, another watercourse left from last winter's rain. She heard them ahead, their catcalls rising and falling, echoing and fading.

The moonlight was romantic and pretty now, a real path shining across the river. It was then that the grandmother saw the aunt sitting, a little way ahead on a tilted flat rock on the edge of a part of the cliff which was higher than the previous places. It was a look-out point, the grandmother thought she remembered it. Behind the aunt, and leaning over her, was a figure indistinguishable in the gathered darkness. The grandmother, pausing for breath, wondered who could stand so still leaning over the aunt and she not turning her gaze from the river to speak to him. The air was fresh with the ever-rising mist and the grandmother could make out the grandsons as they scrambled up on the rock, one each side of the aunt. The tall dark man continued to lean. He seemed not to notice the nephews as they made themselves comfortable, one on each side of the aunt. The grandmother supposed that the aunt would be wearing her usual heavy lisle stockings and her sensible shoes. She wondered for a moment, as she approached slowly, if the leaning figure, the man, the stranger, perhaps not a stranger to the aunt, had noticed the aunt's clothes and if he had noticed, whether he minded them or not.

The grandmother often, with admiration and pleasure, saw young bare legs on bicycles as their owners, apparently without much effort, travelled along the quiet roads from one suburb to the next. She regretted not having noticed her own youthfulness before it passed with such remarkable speed into old age. This was a repeated thought and it was possible that the aunt, walking in seamed stockings and an unfashionable skirt, would notice these young people and have similar feelings of regret over the passing of her own youth. Once in the classroom with her students, the grandmother consoled herself, the aunt would forget what was, after all, only a fleeting moment of regret. Such considerations were unprofitable, the grandmother did not need to remind herself. Even so, there was the recollection, which rose unbidden, of the time when she opened the bathroom door into the fragrant steam just as her eldest daughter (later the aunt) was standing up in the bath reaching for her towel. There she was suddenly grown up, tall, long limbed, graceful and rounded, her skin glowing pink with the hot bath and her own youth. The grandmother had closed the door at once, not saying anything then or later about the beauty of her daughter's body, perhaps because at the time it seemed untouched, untroubled and innocent. Whenever the grandmother recalled this moment she understood that she, herself, had never been rosy pink at the edge of innocence and smooth youthfulness. She had never once considered how she, herself, might have looked as a young woman, either dressed or naked.

The secret paths were formed by the indelible outlines of small garden plots made years ago, edged with river stones and now, without their little crops, were overgrown with coarse grass. The grandmother, treading carefully, advanced slowly along the last remaining path. The man, the stranger, did not alter his position. He leaned as if in supplication towards the aunt. The grandmother felt relieved that there seemed to be no threat in the way in which he stood. She paused once more for comfortable breath and wondered who would be a suppliant to the aunt, and could she be refusing to acknowledge his presence until it suited her to do otherwise. Perhaps this was the undiagnosed fault in the aunt's nature. Perhaps she, as mother, should have seen this earlier and corrected the daughter.

The grandmother recalled the one time the aunt agreed to going on a holiday, a special tour in Europe. The aunt, despising tourists, agreed with reluctance to join a guided tour with an experienced mountaineer; the grandmother could remember some of the place names, Appenzell and Grindelwald and Zermatt in the Swiss Alps. The aunt had returned, apparently unchanged by the experience and silent. The grandmother wondered now, when it was much too late to have such thoughts, whether the aunt's uncompromising attitude, which she could see plainly ahead of her, was the reason that the aunt had simply nothing to say about either the famous mountaineer or the other travellers when she returned from the holiday. She pressed on towards the little group ahead.

The previous year the nephews had eaten the aunt's birthday chocolates; to be more accurate they had each picked out the ones they liked, leaving a ravaged box of chocolate papers, nuts and hard centres. This year, the aunt not wanting her birthday even mentioned, let alone celebrated, there were no chocolates. Of course the grandmother remembered it was the aunt's birthday and clearly she was waiting out the day there along the river bank. There were people who did things like that. They endured. They endured something alone and in silence till it passed.

The grandmother came close to where the aunt and the nephews sat beneath the black shape, which still did not move but continued to lean over them. The grandmother, with an extra strength, marched straight up to confront the stranger. It occurred to her that she might be taking a stupid risk. This unknown man might easily have, as people did have nowadays, a knife. The knife might be at the aunt's back and that might be why she did not turn round to him. The man might mistakenly be thinking that she had money on her. He could have her money, the grandmother told herself. She never went anywhere without her purse. He could have her purse and her pension cheque. He could have her library-book tickets. It would be safer to offer all she had. There was no need for him to strangle her and snatch her purse. She would hold it out to him and tell him he could have it and be off. She would tell him in plain words.

Then the grandmother saw and remembered, just in time, a big old pear tree there at the back of the rock. It was nothing more than a leaning stump now, but substantial for all that the branches had, at different times, been lost to firewood thieves. She did not speak to the stump. She pushed her purse back deep into her pocket and sat down on the edge of the rock to rest and to gaze, as the others were doing, across to the moonlight which trembled now on the calm and dark water. The crushed grass all round the rock gave off a sweetness which comes from hay during the night. There in the peacefulness, in that steady and pleasant orchestration of small night sounds, undisturbed by intruders of the gentle sort, the grandmother came to the conclusion that this river bank had no place and no scale in the road atlas. But, taking the scale given there, this walk, this little journey, even with all its immensity, if you put it into scale, was in fact just a little short of an inch.

Part Two

The Orchard Thieves

'The act of paying is perhaps
the most uncomfortable infliction
that the two orchard thieves
entailed upon us.'

Melville

THE GRANDMOTHER, accompanied by the familiar noise in her head, described by the doctor as vascular, put the seamed sheets and the worn-out army blankets, which she kept for the grandsons, to air round the fire. The little boys were staying the night; 'sleeping over,' they called it. The grandmother said they could stay because the aunt from England was arriving the next day, bringing with her a little girl cousin. The grandsons and this granddaughter had never seen each other, their previous communication being simply crayonned squares and circles, birds' nests scribblings, followed later with scattered fragments of the alphabet and finger-marked drawings, representative to themselves of themselves and their surroundings but, to anyone else, inscrutable.

'You've probably got a major blood vessel too close to the auditory nerve, the nerve of hearing.' The grandmother remembered the doctor's explanation as she listened to her own head and hoped that no one else could hear the effects of this deformity.

This aunt from England was the one who, on receiving a letter from the grandmother, had burst into tears, she wrote back immediately to tell the grandmother. This aunt was the middle sister, the one between the grandsons' mother, the youngest, and the aunt who was the eldest and who was, of course, the *real* aunt. The middle sister, all alone in her London bed-sitting room, had not been able to stop herself from crying when the little dried-up bits of the boronia fell from the pages of the grandmother's letter. In her reply she said that the scent brought back all kinds of things; things like the cracked linoleum by the stove and the way in which the tree, the Japanese pepper, grew into the bathroom window. It was, she wrote, as if she was back in the house with all the doors standing open to the fragrance of the August rains. Suddenly she seemed to remember the bath towels gritty with sand and it was, as if once again, she was barefoot on the boards of the verandah and even about to step off on to the gravel bush track which was the way to school. Her mother (the grandmother) and the two sisters could never know, she added in a postscript splashed with tears, what the scent of the boronia could do to anyone alone in London. It was all so unexpected. And, she had to admit, she had lost her way in the seasons.

There was no father to accompany the middle sister and her little girl on the long journey across the world. The grandmother wondered about her daughter and the little granddaughter she had never seen. She hoped that the real aunt would not be as outspoken as she was inclined to be. And she hoped, above all, that the grandsons would mind their manners, keep their voices down and refrain from bad language and biscuit raids, in any case, to start off with. She had a painful and unwanted recurring memory of her own hands, horribly like claws, snatching the fistfuls of milk arrowroot biscuits from the inadequate, unwashed fingers of the little thieves.

'Rogues!' she said to herself several times a day. At the same time another word, forming in her head, disturbed her. *Confiscating*, that was the word. She felt that she had seized the biscuits with an authority which, at the time, because of the smallness of their hands, seemed particularly unreasonable and unpleasant. All the same, she hoped they would not, straight away, lead the little girl cousin into temptation.

There were times, and this was one of them, when the grandmother wished for an elixir, the kind of magic potion described in ancient legends. It could be something quite simple, she thought, an essence was what she had in mind. She did not want anything which required a cauldron and special herbs and the services of her three daughters for the administration of the treatment. It was not a version of the prescription in the mythology; she was not looking for the return to youthfulness as promised to the daughters of the aging Pelias. That remedy was doomed to failure. During her life she avoided medicines and had never needed to take slimming tablets as other women, she had known, did. She'd even heard it said that some brands of these tablets had actually contained worm eggs.

Her daughters would not be required to be watchful. They would not be expected to administer the elixir. She pictured herself measuring the dose at those particular times when experiencing the full flight and fall of vitality.

The elixir would be in a bottle, dark blue but smooth and not ridged as a poisons bottle is ridged, this being the recognisable warning to anyone who might, when in pain during the night, grab the bottle, in the dark, and, without looking to see what the contents were, drink deeply expecting an instant cure. This dark-blue smooth bottle would look, she imagined, rather like the Milk of Magnesia and the Gripe Water bottles purchased, years ago, for her own babies. These clean blue flasks on the shelf above the sink were always a reassuring sight and she could not have counted the times, at all hours of the day or night, when she had reached for one or the other.

The elixir, the essence, would be honey coloured, aromatic-bitter on the tongue, but sweet and warm when swallowed. The word elixir had magical connotations. It was not simply a matter of wishing to be young again. She had no wish to relive earlier years. She wished for energy and, for good measure, something in the mixture which would clear her mind of anxious thoughts and perhaps prevent her from being forgetful, especially of birthdays and saucepans.

The aunt told the nephews that, yes, they could play in her room for half an hour.

The grandmother with a poem; *These little Limmes, These Eys and Hands which here I find*, and a double bathing on her mind, passed the aunt's partly open door and heard the soft crooning voices accompanying an awesome task.

'Cool, man! Take a look, willya. Unreal!'

'Cool, man! She's got nothing on. Cool.'

The grandsons, unwinding a sari, were crouched on the floor. The sari was orange and green and was decorated with tiny mirrors sewn into the cotton material. The soft whisperings from the seclusion of this special room reminded the grandmother of the gentle and private whisperings of the birds in the river-cliff bushes in the early mornings and, more especially, in the late afternoons, in that particular time as the sun was moving westward, when the grass took on a more intense green and lengthening shadows accompanied those people who were walking there.

Behind What Curtain were ye from me hid so long!

The grandmother, the words on the lips but not spoken, stopped behind the half-closed door and peered, with caution, into the room. The three Indian Ladies stood to one side, in a little group, half turned to each other. They seemed, with their downcast eyes and the exquisite positioning of their little hands and feet, to be confiding perplexities. The fourth, the recipient of much handling and examination was, without her clothes, upside down. The grandmother could, easily, imagine the embroidery of shame on her little cloth face. She could imagine too the eyes of the grandsons darkening with the intensity of their game; their faces pale in contrast to the deep shadows surrounding their eyes and their lips, their expressions changing as they changed when the grandmother or the aunt read aloud to them. She thought, as she listened, that she would never know what they were seeing during either a make-believe game or a story. It was as if they had the ability to inhabit a world so strange at these times that she became anxious, fearing possible unhappiness or cruelty of some sort, in the future, for them. And, even more, she selfishly feared her own loss, should they enter realms which would be closed to her.

'Wow, man! Take a look, willya. No pants.'

'Wow, man. That's right. No pants.'

'Man! her legs is stitched. See? At the top.'

'Yeah, man, she's stitched up all right.'

The coloured cloth of the tiny jacket and sari lay on the floorboards, soon to be followed by a second and third set of garments, till all four dolls, their pink cotton bodies looking very small, were all lined up for further investigation and comparison.

Pausing still outside the door, the grandmother wanted to go into the room. She thought of kneeling down beside the children. She longed to brush their soft hair with her lips. Sometimes she prayed inside herself that they would stay small and clean and good. Wholesome was a better word. For ever.

But this would be ridiculous. She could hear the aunt's scorn. She did not need to imagine what the aunt would say to this kind of prayer or thought. The aunt would tell her that she, the grandmother, would be the first to be worried to death if either of the grandsons failed to eat properly and, because of this, failed to grow and develop. And then, what if they were not able to learn to read and to add up and subtract, to multiply and divide? Even things like riding bicycles and being able to throw and catch a ball, especially a ball falling from a great height, the grandmother knew that they, the children, must go forward to all these things. She always watched, with an unforeseen pleasure, the grandsons running and jumping and swimming. She listened, with the same surprising pleasure, to their hesitant reading and she watched, without them knowing she was watching as they, with rounded blunt scissors, cut out very small pictures from advertisements in magazines; a garden rake, an electric carving knife, a mobile telephone and then several mobile telephones complete with competitive prices. And then, after all their care with cutting, they discarded these pictures and forgot about them. She watched with amusement and trepidation the elder grandson's large handwriting, it was called running writing, becoming small and mean on the page with never a mistake. The handwriting of a mathematician, she thought, or someone in the legal profession.

If she had wisdom at all, she told herself, she must know that she would not be with them for ever and she could not have any idea of what destiny, for want of a better word to cover the dreadful things, might have in store for them. Often she sat, upright and watchful from within, her sewing lying in her lap, as thoughts invaded. Dismissing wars, road accidents, fires and illness, accepting failure in ambition and failure in love she experienced tragedy at closer quarters. A grandson, on the high up river-cliff path, with a misjudged leap landing on a tuft of grass with the substance of the cliff already washed away from below, and the child's body discovered later in a broken heap at the foot of the cliff. And then the second grandson, blindly following the first, meeting with the same terrible fall and, instead of death, a subsequent injury from which there could be no real recovery. She refrained from mentioning these fearful pictures to the aunt, knowing that the aunt would, quite rightly, be impatient saying that such thoughts were negative and could cause harm to the children, making them lose their confidence, could cause them to fall, that sort of thing. The aunt would have no sympathy. Thoughts could fill the mind so quickly, one thought giving way to another, like now outside the aunt's door.

The grandmother wanted, above all, that the grandsons would carry with them, for the rest of their lives, the special things. For example, they would take with them, without really thinking about it and without knowing that they were actually taking anything, the way in which the aunt had always cherished them and considered them before anything else in her life. She had cradled them in her large hands, first one and then the other, as soon as they were born. And she had continued to hold and to treasure them. There would be other things remembered, walks and games, conversations, stories and ideas and, perhaps, even this morning's investigation. The grandmother, pausing still, wondered if she should intervene and say something educational and wise. The little dolls were naked still and the inspection was completed.

'Wow, man. That's it. Neat, eh?'

'Yeah. Neat. Unreal.'

'Yeah. Neat. Unreal. Cool, man.'

There seemed to be no need to embark on an explanation. The grandmother told the grandsons, as she passed the door, to tidy up. She would, she said, fix them both some bread and butter and later they could pick nasturtiums. She would give them a jam jar each. Some flowers in the room she had prepared for the other aunt and the little cousin from England would look very nice, she said.

One grandson, the one with the small handwriting, picked his bunch without leaves, a barbaric little mass of colour bursting at the mouth of the jar. The other made a trailing arrangement all across and over the edges of the dressing table. He had chosen the stalks and the flat green leaves, with only a few of the flowers which provided small, half-hidden splashes of yellow and orange. This grandson was the one who, when guests were inevitable, arranged biscuits from grocers' packets on china plates or he would, sometimes, make a fruit bowl for the table with red and yellow apples, russet pears and the grandmother's own orchard-grown mandarin oranges, their thick skins loose and shining with an excess of the fragrant oil. He would include little touches of purple and green, that delicate balance between bloom and translucence belonging to the skins and the flesh of grapes. Even when at their most expensive, the aunt always said that, in spite of the price, to celebrate his art, his gift, she called it, a few grapes should be included in the shopping.

In spite of the grandmother's persuasion, visitors, rather than spoil the work of art, would abstain from helping themselves to the fruit. As with birthday chocolates which were not consumed by the recipient (the aunt, for example, who no longer wished to celebrate her birthdays), there was a similar sense of duty towards the fruit. It was incumbent on the grandsons, at least it seemed so to the grandmother since they never ate fruit when it was especially peeled and cut up for them, to raid and wreck the splendid bowl leaving pear stalks, apple cores and partly chewed grape-skins discarded, reminiscent of the ravaged remains of a chocolate box left with the torn wrappings, nuts and hard centres, in two neat little heaps just as if, the grandmother thought, a couple of possums had enjoyed a night out and a late supper.

It was necessary, it seemed, that this kind of thieving should take place under cover of darkness at such times when the grandmother and the aunt and their visitors had moved to sit out the evening on the verandah. The grandsons, pushing aside their seamed sheets, would creep along the passage, their thin feet light as paper on the floor and then, crouched double, they would reach the table and close their equally light and competent fingers carefully round an apple or a pear, a mandarin orange or two, not forgetting the expensive grapes and, with the same soft sound as of a page, torn from a book and drifting to settle on the floorboards, would return to their small beds, low and close to the floor, to share between them the proceeds of the raid.

The grandmother accepted this raiding and wrecking. Fruit, she thought, like biscuits, had to be stolen. The little girl cousin, she understood, would come under this influence if she did not already have it within her. Of course, the grandsons could not continue to be robbers. This raiding and wrecking belonged only to childhood. It was all a part of the miracle and the illumination of survival which the grandsons, as they asserted themselves in their quest for living, kept adding to her own experience and understanding. Never mind if it was rather late in her life.

She would read *Robinson Crusoe* to them. All children steal something, she reminded herself. All children should have *Robinson Crusoe* read aloud to them. The impressions from childhood reading perhaps last longer than any other, so deeply do they reach the imagination. Because, when words in the telling voice, or, in their leaping up from the printed page, are suddenly understood where previously there was no understanding, they, these words, hold an everlasting magic.

The grandsons could not continue to be robbers. People should not steal, the grandmother would make her lesson clear, perhaps on a rug in the garden, she thought, forgetting her previous failures. She liked, when she remembered these failures, to think of them as being only *apparent*. After all, who was to know what went into a child's mind, and when. The child himself might not know until very much later.

The grandmother took the book out into the garden. Long shadows lay across the uncut grass of the little orchard. The grandmother said that the parrots were quarrelling over the best places for roosting. She said that parrots, like humans, always wanted the best for themselves. She told the grandsons that now they were old enough to know better, they should not steal. She explained that Defoe, the author of *Robinson Crusoe*, wrote about characters who were like real people and had very hard lives. If they raided and stole, it was because they had to live. They used their wits, their quick thoughts and their nimble fingers and legs in order to survive. She spelled the word *survive* and said it was a new word for them. They should learn a new word every day, she said. *Similarly* (another new word which she spelled for them), similarly men should not use guns, they should not shoot unless it was to get meat for dinner. Towards the end of the book, she told the grandsons, Robinson Crusoe is not really a likeable man and it would not matter, just now, if they did not read to the end of his adventures. She was going to read to them, she said, from the part where he is shipwrecked and how he manages to save some things from the ship and build himself a little hut on an island. He builds a fence, a palisade he calls it, because it is made of pickets banged into the sand. He has to live all alone as there are no other people on the island.

June 26th, the grandmother read, *took my gun . . .*

I killed a she goat and with much difficulty got it home and broiled some of it and ate . . .

While the grandmother was spelling *palisade* for the grandsons she remembered suddenly that she had said she would make a creamy potato soup for the arrival of the middle sister and the little cousin the next day.

> Where have ye been? Behind
> What Curtain were ye from me hid so long!
> Where was? in what Abyss, my Speaking Tongue?

The poem came back to the grandmother with the double bathing. The grandsons, kneeling in the bath, held torn-up pieces of an old towel over their eyes while the grandmother washed and rinsed their heads till they looked like the heads of baby seals, round and small, shining wet and sleek.

> These little Limmes,
> These Eys and Hands which here I find
> These rosie Cheeks wherwith my Life begins,

The grandmother, reflecting, could see by their obedience and compliance that the bath was less of an ordeal than Robinson Crusoe's survival. It was, of course, possible that they were going over in their minds the examination earlier of the Indian Ladies, or were simultaneously hatching some plot which would reveal itself in due course.

The soup, that was the next thing she must think about. One soup in the mind leads to another. The Indian dolls were a gift to the aunt from a visiting educationalist, a most refined man with slender beautiful hands. He clearly admired the aunt very much and the grandmother saw, with longing, the intellectual approach so very possible and yet, entirely, because of circumstances, impossible.

Sometimes it seemed to the grandmother that she often made soup for an occasion which presented difficulties of the heart-breaking kind. In any case the mother could not be expected to discover the right mate for the daughter. The aunt herself would be hurt if she had any idea of her mother's thoughts.

The grandsons, ransacking the grandmother's sewing basket, found an old tape measure. The grandmother, standing just inside the front-room door, waited with patience while the grandsons measured the height, off the floor, of the little beds which had been made up for them. They estimated that each bed was four inches above the floorboards, but both had to agree the beds were, in fact, eight inches off the floor. Before they could measure anything else the grandmother removed the hot-water bottles, saying that she would take away the measuring tape if they did not get into bed immediately. She said that she thought it would be a useful sum to convert the inches into centimetres. She told them she would set it out for them first thing in the morning.

The grandmother heard, with satisfaction, the small sighings of comfort and oncoming sleep as the grandsons, sliding into the tightly tucked-in beds, felt the warmth which awaited them.

The mind of man is fram'd even like the breath
And harmony of music. There is a dark
Invisible workmanship that reconciles
Discordant elements, and makes them move
In one society . . .

The grandmother, later in the evening, looked up from Wordsworth's *Prelude.* She liked, she told the aunt, the fact that the long poem was also called *Growth of a Poet's Mind.* She told the aunt that instead of lemonade or milo she would have a rum jungle.

I have no idea, the grandmother said to the aunt later, why I said I would have a rum jungle. She wondered why she had asked for one. She had, in fact, been thinking about Wordsworth's conscience in connection with a small boat, and about her own nose. This last thought became the stronger and she was convinced that, as she became older, more elderly, she would be all nose. She thought this was applicable to the aunt also, but she did not mention this when the aunt finally came back into the room having, at last, made up her mind what to wear.

The grandmother remembered when the aunt was about nine years old (and of course, not an aunt then), that she, the grandmother had looked at the aunt across the table saying that she thought the aunt would, one day, be a teacher because she had a severe nose. She remembered too that there had been no consolation suitable to offer after saying this. Even changing the severity of the nose into a musician's nose had not worked. The aunt's two younger sisters had perfect noses in comparison but they lacked everything the aunt had, especially the music.

The aunt, the grandmother knew, was only at ease with other people when nursing her cello. The aunt, when she was invited anywhere, would have preferred to dress in the formal white blouse and the black skirt, quite plain, cut and tailored, it could be said, for the concert platform either at the school or in the town hall. The grandmother listened, as usual, to the aunt's indecision about clothes. She heard the wardrobe door protesting, creaking, almost closing by itself. And then the savage sound, the noisy movement of coat hangers being pushed back into the space behind the other door which did not open. Then there was the deep sigh, which was the forerunner of yet another change of blouse or jacket, and then the heavy footsteps, to and fro, across the floorboards and the familiar shudder of the chest as the drawers were, one after the other, pulled open and pushed shut. The grandmother understood all this all too well. She felt she was partly to blame. For wasn't it true of herself? Often she wished she could be dressed in her comfortable nightgown and slippers. In fact she always felt that she looked her best then, with the pastel colours and the ruffles of lace at the neck and wrists. Her plaid slippers, too, were really quite smart enough for visiting or a concert.

This evening it was not a concert and the aunt was not going to school to teach. There was no problem about her teaching clothes, these had been decided upon, once and for all, years ago. This was a troublesome evening, a mid-term social occasion, starting too late in any case. Though the grandmother told the aunt that she had no idea why she asked for a rum jungle, she did suppose, she said, that it suggested a lifetime of looking forward to parties and might create a mood or a sophisticated knowledge of hilarious behaviour, in itself a good preparation for going out against one's wishes. The rum jungle, though she had no idea what it might contain, seemed like a nice thought.

The grandmother, in the absence of the wild drink, settled for a sherry and looked, with approval at the aunt's dress which, though it did not quite suit her, was a garment of good quality.

The aunt's hands, when she gave the grandmother her drink, were dreadfully cold. The grandmother restrained herself from remarking on the hands, on the dress and on the forthcoming evening. Instead she sipped her sherry rather too quickly and wondered why women never saw themselves as a complete whole. They never saw the whole person, the general effect of the complete person. The overall appearance, the grandmother wanted to say, was what mattered; the blending of the colours and the suitability of the cloth for the occasion and, above all, it was the expression of composure, serenity was perhaps a better word, in the eyes which made all the difference between being well or badly dressed. Women, she thought, and she would have liked to speak of this, only saw themselves in bits and, as well, saw only the faults in themselves. They were always conscious of the physical fault, the extra chin, the wry mouth, eyes too small or too close together, a flat nose, an ugly nose, fat legs or legs which were too thin and had no shape, lifeless drab hair, the list could go on, and they never, these women, they never saw serenity in their own expressions because of the anxiety reflected in the last-minute glancings in mirrors. The eyes they saw were forever worried and accompanied by small but deep frowns. And, in any case, it was not the physical details or the clothes and the accessories which mattered most. It was the personality which made the difference between being badly dressed or well dressed.

Green and a russet brown, the softer colours of the spring and the autumn, were the best colours for the aunt. A pleasant tweed combining this softness was in the grandmother's mind. A good quality, quiet tweed was both elegant and consoling . . .

All this, the grandmother thought, was because of the rum jungle, one idea, one small thought or memory, one imagined thing led so quickly to another. And, of course it, the drink, was only a sherry, a small one and too sweet, to keep the aunt company before she had to go out.

The books in her room were too heavy, the aunt said. She told the grandmother that the crack in the plaster was deep and the shelf would pull away from the wall. The grandmother moved her books, putting them all along the mantelpiece which was certainly the best place for them, as the chimney had always seemed, to her, to be the most substantial part of the house. The photographs, the aunt said, would be perfectly all right on the shelf.

Rogues, you could call them rogues *and* thieves, both of them, the grandmother said to herself every morning when she looked along her little gallery of pictures. Every morning the grandmother was greeted by the grandsons as they, in their progress all the way from their cradles to their present size, looked back at her from their new place in her room. The round face of the first grandson stared now with the heavy expression which accompanies the expectation of responsibility, whereas the second grandson, with the lamp light creating a contemporary halo on his fair hair, had, while the latest picture was being taken, tilted his head forward, causing his smile to be enlarged and twisted into the carefree grin of the younger brother. This grin was well matched with the cornflower blue of his eyes. These eyes, the grandmother recalled them often without meaning to think of them, which he, at one time, refused to close even when he was precarious on the verge of sleep. It made no difference whether she padded to and fro across the floorboards with him in her arms or if she sat rocking him, crooning during the long night. She sang her lullaby then in that particular voice which, cracked with age, disappeared into a whisper which had no melody. She sang on in this way till the whisper cracked and the voice came back husky and with an entirely different song. And all the time the penetrating blue eyes, tiny crystals of blue ice, continued to gaze from beneath the lids. He seemed to watch or scrutinize every movement she might make or every thought she might have.

The grandmother frequently offered thanks, perhaps to a God resembling her own grandfather, for the blessing of sleep. She did not dwell too long on the rapidly changing expressions of the children. As the years heaped up on them the little glances of shy hope and tenderness almost vanished from their features. And their home-made baby clothes, suitable for their daily explorations of the front gardens and the water meters along the streets, gave way to standard shorts of a tough grey twill and to thick, machine-knitted school jumpers, from which their thin stalk-like necks appeared all the more vulnerable because of the crude bulky blue and red collars, also machine knitted. These garments were complete with buttonholes (machine made), and cheap buttons which were never fastened properly. Usually there was an extra button at the top of the thick woollen facing and an empty buttonhole at the bottom.

The grandsons, or nephews if you were thinking of the aunt, were more substantial as the days went by and often they were silent. If they cried at all it was a silent crying with the mouth drawn downwards and square, with only a slight trembling of the lips and chin. The eyes overflowed, as if in secret with little outward show, suggesting a despair of crying within. And then the breath would be drawn in, with scarcely heard sobs causing the shoulders to heave and to curve forward. It was a developed way of crying brought about by conventional repression of any outward show of distress, unspoken, but expected of them. It replaced forever the shrill sounds of protest which both brought into the world with them, and which suggested that each one, in turn, was anticipating the hardships and the sorrows of human life, beginning with that first handling - as if by the scruff of the neck, the wailing and the kicking of the frog-like, thin legs ignored - as the small body was held, helpless, above the basin of warm water for the first ritual, that of being washed.

The grandmother, whenever she looked along her little gallery of rogues and thieves, knew at once that they would, during their lives, do something perfect and noble and wonderful and something absolutely appalling. Sometimes during the early hours of the morning, perhaps after a night of wind and rain with the clouds wildly caressing the moon, or, like now, when she was sitting up in her dressing gown waiting for the aunt to come home, she pictured herself sitting, crouching and shivering, over the telephone trying to contact the police or a crisis centre or, failing both, a grandmother's support group. She knew that these days it was more difficult (and this would no doubt get worse) to get help of any kind in an emergency. For wasn't it fairly recently, after a storm, when she had no electricity for two days she finally managed to report the damage and a young woman's voice at the other end of the telephone kept repeating that she was sorry she could not take a message as her *computer was down*. The grandmother asked her, 'But dear, couldn't you write a message on a bit of paper?' Before she could give her name and address the far-away reedy voice explained that it was not possible to take a message as there was nothing to write on and nothing to write with.

What would happen if she had something terrible to report? Steadily, the grandmother's fears increased with this sense of isolation . . . and here she reprimanded herself. She was sitting comfortably in her dressing gown, waiting up for the aunt, and both grandsons were asleep in their beds. The awful thing they were going to do had not yet entered their heads. She would be careful not to let slip her stupid flights of imagination to the aunt. All the same, she would, in her prayers to her own old grandfather (funny how he turned up so much now), ask for protection for the grandsons, especially with the little cousin expected so soon. The little girl, being brought up in England, would not know the grandsons and their ways. She did not want her own small orchard thieves to bear for the rest of their lives the penalty, the endless act of paying, this legacy left from the original Orchard Thieves, for ever.

Naturally she would never say a word of this to anyone, especially not to the aunt and certainly not to the grandsons' mother or to the middle daughter who was, at this time, on her way, on the long journey, bringing the innocent little cousin straight into the lovable iniquitous world of the grandsons.

Often when she was alone and waiting for the aunt to return from something which might have been, years ago, an excitement or, more likely now at the present time, an incredibly dull few hours which would leave the aunt almost in tears and with a headache lasting far too long, she would recall an intellectual awakening which the aunt, when she was still a university student and not an aunt, experienced. A lecturer, handsome and advanced in age, had a charming scholarly approach. He had, as well, an attractive wife and four children. It was clear to the grandmother that he, during a dinner party at his own house, turned instinctively to the quiet plain girl, the student with intelligent eyes, and at once involved her for the whole evening in the intimacy of a penetrating literary conversation. His wife, a perfect hostess allowed, even encouraged this. It became the first of many such occasions. The grandmother had to understand that painful, though it was, she had to warn and protect her daughter when she, of necessity, would have to give up the pleasure of the masculine, more than friendly attack and attention accompanying his method of teaching. Reliving the pain of drawing a daughter away and out of an all encapsulating world of being chosen by the mentor, the grandmother knowing that such thoughts were unprofitable, reached for the three-miles-to-one-inch maps. All the towns and cities were included in the book of maps, even the smallest villages were marked as were rivers and forests, ancient castles, battlefields and roads. The first-class roads were shown in red and the second class roads were blue. The relative importance of the uncoloured roads was indicated as they were drawn, by the width of the parallel lines. Footpaths were shown with dotted lines only. Footpaths thus represented, the grandmother knew, were not necessarily evidence of a right of way. A farmer, a landowner, she would say to herself, had every right to turn trespassers off his land. She thought of the Penn Road going south-west from the industrial part of the Midlands to Bewdley, a small country town on the River Severn and wrapped at the edges in the Wyre Forest. All round Bewdley, behind the shops and the houses, there were little lanes with gates and stiles, overhung with leafy trees. She and her own sisters, on holiday there when they were children, discovered one little lane after another. It was not hard now to think about the lanes, even though they were in another country and probably did not exist any more. She recaptured often the feeling of being half hidden in the tall grass and the cow parsley along the hedgerows and the ditches. Then there was the warm sweet scent of the cut grass in the hay fields . . .

All this belonged to an earlier time in her life. It would be of no use to walk there now alone. A pretty or a grand landscape was of no use if you were alone and lonely. She had learned this early on in her life, the aunt too was acquainted with this truth. They both knew but never spoke of it, that it was nothing, it *came* to nothing, for example, when walking alone as a stranger, just visiting, to find the path, unexpectedly, to the sea. And this is what they would be doing if they went back to the country they had left or to some new place separately.

There were three places where the grandmother might have left her spectacles. It was better to lose them, as she had this evening, when the aunt was out and the grandsons were in bed. The aunt seemed, every time, in the all encompassing silence which accompanied the grandmother's desperate and wordless searching, to sense this particular loss and to be disturbed by it. As she moved cushions and opened books, the grandmother prepared herself for any unpleasant outcome from the school party. There was to be some music, after all, she remembered, the aunt had at the last moment taken her cello. A recital would relieve the evening, the thought was consoling. Unless, of course, some new member of staff, a brash young woman, with a prepared clever and amusing anecdote from her musical career, had upstaged the aunt completely with both the little speech and the subsequent performance. The aunt was at an age when something of this sort could be expected. It was not hard to imagine the headmaster almost fainting with delight at the sight of the young violinist's knee-length boots and her shining long hair, with the fringe causing the partly hidden eyes to be tantalising rather than simply restless and discontented.

Reprimanding herself the grandmother found her spectacles at last between the ragged pages of the English maps. Her imaginings, out of control, were harmless but could be a nuisance. Hearing the aunt's small car turning on the gravel, the grandmother with almost schoolgirlish haste put herself to bed and was there on the pillows, reading quietly, all ready to turn with a smile when the aunt should put her head round the door to exchange the usual words of comfort which always passed between them.

The grandmother understood that her own thoughts were often unbridled and it was the ensuing worried state which kept her awake. She remembered a book, the title and the author now forgotten; in this book a nun tells a sleepless and possibly unhappy woman that if she kept the name of Jesus on her lips throughout the night sleep would come.

Jesus, oh Jesus. Gentle Jesus, *forgive us our trespasses ...*

The middle daughter and the little cousin would be arriving in the late afternoon the next day. Supposing the grandsons locked the little cousin in the wardrobe, supposing they lost the key of the wardrobe and what if they went, one each side of her, down the slope to the creek where there were deep holes and slippery edges of mud ... The grandsons might not understand that they were rough, rougher than ... And then there could be a snake ...

Jesus, oh Jesus, *forgive us our trespasses as we forgive them that trespass against us.*

Jeezuss, Jeez Ah! Jeez squeeze, the grandsons, not knowing, might say their own prayer.

In her purse the grandmother had fourteen lending-library tickets.

'Take one,' she said. 'Most of these people are

dead,' she explained, offering the intimacy of the bulging compartments of her purse to a stranger who, undecided and holding books in both hands, was standing in front of the shelves in the fiction section. 'Please do have a ticket,' the grandmother said. She went on to say that she knew how awful it was to get all the way home only to discover that the books were familiar, having been read before. This way, she explained, with an extra book or two there was more chance of having something completely fresh to read.

On the way home the grandmother thought about the special kind of wealth there was in the possession of library-book tickets. They were reassuring and steady like the pension cheque. She never went anywhere without her purse. You could never know in advance what the day had in store. There might come a time when it would be necessary to offer all she had to appease an intruder. She knew of women who spread crumpled and torn newspapers all round their beds every night so that they would hear the intruder coming closer. Or, she might be held at knife point by someone in the street. She would offer all she had in her purse, small change, pension cheque and the library-book tickets. There would be absolutely no need for a villain to either strangle or stab her in order to snatch her purse. She would hold it out to him and tell him he could have it and be off. She would tell him this in plain words. The library-book tickets might even make a changed man of him, especially if he had never had a chance to use a public lending library during a life with all the deprivation brought about by being on the run.

The grandmother, remembering the cream soup she intended to make for the arrival of the middle daughter and the little grandchild, quickened her step. It was not possible to hurry the preparation of this soup. She recalled the time, lately, when she had forgotten a vital step in the making of the special soup and was about to pour the failure into the sink when the aunt, preventing this, rebuked her saying, 'Well, so what if it curdled. Why make such a fuss, it's eatable the way it is.'

Somewhere, in her head, she could still hear the snort of indignation in the aunt's voice. One soup led to another and she remembered the time when she served another soup from the deep pot which simmered at the back of the wood stove. Fortunately it was a vegetable soup and was therefore suitable for the Indian gentleman who did not eat meat. There was a certain uneasiness which went with the memory of this particular meal. The gentleman was an educationalist from India. He was visiting schools and the aunt, taking pity on him, feeling that he should not be left to face the evening and the evening meal all alone in the hotel, brought him home. It was during the shy silence of the meal that the grandmother suffered a secret thought, an uneasiness. She recollected all too clearly the bone boiled for the stock, which was the foundation for the soup but which she never regarded as being meat. If she had been capable of blushing she would have presented a scarlet face at the table as she remembered this glistening ball and socket, this hip bone from which the best beef steak came, and wasn't that the same as the sacred cow? Naturally she did not mention any of this, but kept her gaze on the slender hands of the guest as he handled his table napkin and his soup spoon. She surprised herself, as she saw the smooth long fingers fondle the cloth, by imagining the way in which his hands could caress the aunt, her cheek, her neck and her shoulder, but quickly she stopped the thought and made herself think instead of the shining healthy, well-fed curves of the dark woman, who was the rightful recipient of his sensuality and was bravely the mother of his six children, expecting the seventh and awaiting his safe return.

The Indian dolls were a present, an expression of thanks. They came with some very thin sheets of paper on which the areas they represented and the meaning of the different colours and ornaments were described. He liked the continuity, he wrote in his delicate handwriting, and the sense of handing on the traditions of the past as well as the idea of present-day communication across the great continents of the world. He had enjoyed very much his time with them both and would have liked to discuss literature, English literature, with them at length.

The grandmother and the aunt, after his visit, told each other they were touched by his faith in Kipling, Galsworthy and Charles Kingsley and his ability to quote from them, the grandmother in particular, as these names belonged so much more to her own education and reading. The Indian dolls occupied a top shelf in the aunt's room. Whenever the grandmother saw the dolls, in passing, she felt she was interrupting them in some confidence or other. She remembered as well, repeatedly, the white cuffs and the aristocratic wrists of the owner of these shirt cuffs, which so correctly emerged half an inch beyond the sleeves of his jacket. She easily recalled the pleasure, in spite of the temporary uneasiness over the soup, of the meal time as if it had been transformed by the same magic which had transformed a room and a meal during a moment in her childhood when, by mistake, instead of drinking from her own enamelled cup, she had picked up a glass of water, set out carefully for a guest, and while drinking she had seen the room changed, as if in a dream, through the ice-cold water and the polished glass. This vision, this transformation and the suggested possibilities of being surrounded by beauty had accompanied her throughout her life. Occasions such as the visit from the Indian professor of education remained easily within comparison. She had no way of knowing whether any examples of the wonder of beauty would come to the grandsons. She supposed that they would accept and take beauty, like the soft pulse of the heartbeat, for granted. And there was, as well, the chance that they would, one day, be aware of it with a deep sense of responsibility and awe.

The grandmother, in speech, always referred to the public lending library, the district hospital, the municipal swimming baths and the lady doctor. It did not matter to her that no one else expressed themselves in this way.

Senile warts, the doctor told her. The grandmother noticed that he hesitated over the word 'senile'. The lady doctor, had it been her turn in the surgery, would not have shown any such hesitation. 'Senile warts,' he said, 'nothing to worry about, just don't knock them.' He helped her to draw her sleeves down. The grandmother told him that she did not mind the word 'senile'. There were words far worse, she said, terminal, for example. Some days, though she did not speak of this, the grandmother woke early and immediately began to feel afraid of her own old age and all the things which might be wrong with her; splayed fingers and the ridging of the finger nails could be an indication of something hidden within her person. But the warts were enough for one visit.

It was time to go for the bus. The aunt, who was at school, had already arranged to be able to leave early in the afternoon to fetch the middle sister and the little girl niece from the airport. The grandsons, accompanying the grandmother on her errands, carrying potatoes and leeks, studied the comics in the doctor's waiting room. When the bus stopped on the corner, the grandsons were the first on to it.

The grandmother had not meant to go to the doctor but, finding she needed a prescription and, remembering the dark rough spots on her skin and the way in which people looked at them and turned away as if shaking their heads with some dismal knowledge, thought it was time for a consultation. The doctor was always reassuringly dismissive. One could live for ever in perfect health because of this.

The grandsons, with their own engines, sat as close behind the driver as possible and moved through the gear changes with appropriate sounds. Meanwhile the grandmother rested. It was a short journey which she enjoyed. Almost at once they left the street with shops and houses and followed a road between summer-bleached paddocks left, for the time being, between the developing suburbs of houses and gardens. The grandmother, as they approached a certain group of trees, always thought of the particular place in the Brahms German Requiem where the soprano voice rises singing:

And ye now therefore have sorrow:
but I will see you again, and your heart
shall rejoice, and your joy no man taketh from you . . .

The passage was, she thought, from St John, chapter 16, verse 22. The soprano seemed to sing through the trees, through the restless foliage and up over the sunlit tree tops for miles, on and on. The voice was, forever in her memory of it, sweet and tender and, at the same time, sure and sustained. The grandmother thought it was lovely music. When she was on her way home, like now, on this short bus journey, she liked to think of this music stored secretly above the trees. It seemed to her to come from the shining edges of the clouds and it was as if carried in the wind. She would describe it one day to the grandsons. It was the kind of music she would like at her funeral. She would remember to tell the aunt.

As well, there were among the psalms the seven

penitential psalms written in lyrical poetry, a rhythmical cadence expressing joy, sorrow, anxiety, hope, spiritual distress and a kind of triumphant state of mind. A few lines, the same ones always, came to her frequently during these journeys, one from the sixth psalm:

O Lord, heal me; for my bones are vexed . . .

and from psalm thirty-two:

Thou art my hiding place; thou shalt preserve me from trouble;
Thou shalt compass me about with songs of deliverance . . .

The grandmother had listed the following psalms of penance; the number thirty-eight, number fifty-one, number 102, number 130 and number 143. She thought that the number thirty-eight and the number fifty-three, when spoken of by their numbers, these two sounded as if they could be trams or buses. She learned by heart the more musical and optimistic lines, those written with a special choice and elevation of language, laden with thought, and which could be on her lips briefly before it was time to tell the grandsons to apply their brakes and climb down after her, following the safety of her body off the bus.

Back home once more she, occupied with her thoughts and without her spectacles, peeled the potatoes and chopped up the washed leeks for her soup. She moved with method through the afternoon from one thing to the next. The younger grandson, his blue eyes cutting the stillness of the hour, came into the kitchen holding in his small hand her mislaid spectacles. The grandmother, grateful, suggested that to fill the time, since everything was in readiness for the arrival of the little girl grandchild, they should stack the fallen edges of the wood heap. She left her vegetables to show them how to do this. She was surprised that the exertion did not change the noise in her head. It remained as steady as a well-serviced and regulated water pump. The grandsons never paid any attention to the disfiguring marks of old age or the warts when she rolled up her sleeves. She supposed that these things, as far as they were concerned, were simply a well-known part of her.

The wood heap reminded her that she often thought that people stacked up more firewood than they would use in their lifetime. She remembered from her childhood enormous wood heaps. An inheritance, she supposed firewood could be considered an inheritance. She watched the grandsons clambering like monkeys over the logs. Thieves, she said to herself. Firewood and Fruit Thieves. She remembered their mouths stuffed full of unripe fruit, picked too soon and wasted. The act of paying, for orchard thieves, it was possible to smile in retrospect, the act of paying was in fact a most uncomfortable infliction as if passed on directly from the original thieves though, in the case of grandsons, their payment was in the form of stomach cramps during the long night. Up to the present time an innocence prevailed.

The little cousin, the small granddaughter possibly dressed in a sophisticated way with matching precocious talk and behaviour might, in fact, steal from the grandsons. This was a fresh thought accompanied by the idea of a little girl's flat childish body trying to support a silly mother's choice of clothing. Clothes imitating a grown-up woman's garments. The middle daughter had shown, at one time, that she could be very silly.

What does it mean? the Indian professor had asked that time at the dinner table. He consulted his small notebook, it was a phrase in contemporary literature. 'Fur coat and no knickers,' he said. The words in his accent sounding quaint to the point of being ridiculous.

'I would need to see it in context,' the aunt said then. She glanced at the offered page. 'The English language has problems,' she said with her quiet smile. The grandmother, not knowing how an explanation could be found, busied herself with cups and saucers, the Indian professor having said he would like some tea.

'It is a reference,' the aunt said, making a clinical approach, 'the phrase suggests that the woman being described is wearing an expensive showy outer garment and, being without undergarments, is not modest. Her demeanour suggested by the phrase is carelessly provocative. The phrase,' the aunt said, 'would be a part of a general well-known impression of an adventuress.' The Indian gentleman nodded.

The grandmother's own explanation, 'that girl's no better than she should be,' was stored somewhere inside her head. She kept it there, knowing that it would be too confusing for someone unfamiliar with certain figures of speech.

The grandmother, supported by a savage magnificence of thoughts - each one storming in after the one before - began to fill the bath with hot water. She longed to clean the little granddaughter. She wanted immediately to throw away the small articles of grimy nylon underwear, the lace in particular was disgusting. She wanted to throw away the vulgar dress with its out-of-place sophistication of style and, above all, she wanted to wash away the unwashed dirty little girl smell. Her hair too, she would wash that and comb out all the tangles. It was a sort of ritual bath she had in mind, a wash to overcome the sense of separation, as if the physical handling of the little girl would bring both herself and the child towards an intimacy of innocence and unconditional fondness. This, at their first meeting, had been missing.

The house was standing open to the evening. There was the appearance of precarious restraint, as when a storm gathering over the river causes the wind-powered waves to alter the whole appearance of the normally placid and gleaming water. It was as when musical notes are held in place and cautiously balanced, before the conflict of discord which becomes, in resolution, part of the harmony.

'I've lost my way in the seasons,' the middle sister, in accents cherished carefully all the way from London, wailed. 'Poor darling little house,' she cried, 'I've come *Home*.' She walked through the small rooms. '*Little House*,' she said. 'You are still here! My dear, dear little House.'

The aunt, silent in her look and in her turning aside, accused the middle sister of platitudes. Meaningless remarks, she would have said if she had voiced her thoughts. It was clear that the middle sister woke up every morning, as many people did, uttering banal phrases. These people had whole conversations all day long which consisted of one meaningless remark being replied to safely by another, so that, in fact, nothing was really said or felt.

'Travel shock,' the grandmother, by the bathroom door, warned. 'It's travel shock, that's all.' The grandmother, keeping watch on the hot tap, was nervous. She did not want the visit to be troubled in any way. She would have liked to take the middle daughter in her arms and the little granddaughter as well and bath them both. Both seemed 'shop soiled' in some way, as if dirtied by their experiences. Particularly she did not want criticism or harsh words to be spoken. In spite of a certain brightness, a vivacity increased by full scarlet lips and unnatural eye lashes and fingernails, the middle daughter had deep hollows in her cheeks and dark heavy circles round her eyes which were bright but unsmiling and anxious. Her clothes too, the grandmother thought, were cheap and ugly, a pathetic attempt towards the fashionable. She thought her middle daughter looked big and clumsy in a particular way and she wondered why this was, since the middle one had always been the graceful one, the pretty one, a dancer. She turned off the hot tap and stepped outside to select the special stumpy little logs for the stove. The creamy soup simmered. The soup plates were put to warm. The roasting meat and the potatoes needed a good half an hour more. The grandmother was set on bathing the children before dinner.

In the fading light the grandmother saw the middle sister on the edge of the youngest sister's marriage. The man and the woman, the father and the mother of the grandsons, invited over especially for this dinner, stood together as one person, engrossed, a symbol of parenthood, in their children's game. The grandsons spread across the rough grass of the yard, the little cousin, quickly knowing her place, included, were playing what they called cricket. One boy held the bat and the other threw the ball, he threw hard as boys do. The little cousin ran after the ball. Sometimes the small ball, falling from a great height, was caught. The father shouted corrections, the father, his chest swelling, became the sportsman, the grand coach of all sport. The father shouted praise and he shouted encouragement.

Suddenly the grandmother understood the awkward appearance of the middle daughter. The old clothes and the superficial attempt at a cheap smartness were, she saw now, completely connected with the horrors of family life, the middle daughter's own phrase when she left for a different life in England years ago.

'A pregnant lesbian uproar back in London, source of quotation unknown,' the aunt in a low voice, surprised the grandmother, forcing her to understand quickly, at once, that there must have been, beyond her knowledge and imagination, a turning away from one friendship to another, possibly, almost certainly, with unbearable grief and the inability to separate with grace. The word heartache came to mind swiftly and full of pain.

The grandsons, unaware of anything except themselves, kneeling in their warm bath, covered their eyes with bits of torn-up towel, while the grandmother soaped their heads.

The aunt, adding small logs to the fire, handed small glasses of sherry to the guests.

The grandmother let her mind drift. Suffering was suffering, never mind whose pain it was. Even the one who caused pain suffered. She thought of the imagined bed-sitting room in London and the balance of responsibility in what was now called relationship. It was, after all, a world of couples, in spite of people saying they wanted something they called 'their own space'. Many young women, she thought, when they were no longer young might well regret having their freedom earlier only to face lonely years later. Trust was what mattered. Trust in another person. The middle daughter's petulant mouth would cake her glass with lipstick, another thought pushed aside the previous one. The aunt did not tolerate easily lipstick on cups and glasses. She could hear the aunt adding another small log to the fire. She could hear her topping up the sherry glasses. She could hear the silence.

Suddenly there was a flash of pink flesh and tangled hair. With an accurate leap and a flailing of arms the little granddaughter, as if knowing her place still, was all at once in the bath standing between the grandsons posed, with her legs apart and her arms held up like a dancer about to take some graceful and complicated steps. The grandsons sat in the water looking up at her as she, full of laughter, looked down to them. The grandmother, whose intention had been to have fresh clean water for the little girl's bath, quickly soaped the child's head and body before she, the entailer of infliction, could squat and roll in the water.

The grandmother sat up late at her window looking into and through the dark foliage of her trees. She was looking westward and it seemed that the heavy clouds in the sky were illuminated from the remnants of a fiery sunset for a longer time than usual. It seemed to her that she was looking from her present life into some other mysterious place beyond. Earlier the soft to and fro of the bird voices in the river-cliff bushes reminded her of the gentle voices of the grandsons when, in the seclusion of the aunt's bedroom they undressed her little collection of Indian Ladies. Talking softly, as if persuading and cajoling the diffident dolls, they unwound the brightly coloured and beaded little garments, exclaiming at the length of the winding cloths and the tiny ornamental mirrors minutely stitched into the materials. The dolls did not wear any underclothes.

Fur coat and no knickers, the aunt, with patience and delicacy, had explained the literary cliche to the Indian professor. Perhaps the cliche was applicable to the middle daughter. Speculation was not profitable.

'They can't stay here. They can't, you must see that. For a holiday, yes, but that's all.' The aunt's voice persistent, tired and anxious, long after the house was in the silence of sleep. The grandmother heard in her head the aunt, on the verge of tears. She longed to go into the aunt's room to finish the conversation and to comfort her. It was, after all, the aunt's home as much as it was her own and the aunt was right when she insisted that such an extension of the household would bring discord and very little harmony. The aunt was right too when she reminded the grandmother and herself of the grandmother's age.

The grandmother knew she must think of some way of speaking to the middle daughter. It was not possible to tell a daughter that she could not come home. She must explain to the aunt that the small afflictions of daily living could be overcome. She felt they must be overcome. They were only temporary discomforts and annoyances. It was the unseen things, the real feelings and the deep needs, which were more important. And then there was the unborn baby, the grandmother was unable to erase from her thoughts the recent memory of the brittle smile, the red lips drawn back over the teeth, as the middle sister stood watching during the game and trying to look as if she was an established part of the family. It was then that the grandmother saw, from the awkwardness of the clothes and the tired way of standing, taking the weight first on one foot and then on the other, the advanced pregnancy imperfectly hidden. The owner of this condition would know only too well that it must be revealed soon. The grandmother recalled easily the dull ache in the overtired body during the final weeks.

It was the unseen things which were the more important. How would it be possible, apart from the impossibility of turning away one's own daughter, to turn away, as well, the continuation of the eternal in life, a child who was about to be born.

The aunt, the grandmother knew, when faced with the words, 'how should we live?', would not dispute the question or the answer.

It was easier, when reading a poem to prefer the imagery and the description and to overlook the depths of the observation. The aunt, when she was reading aloud, always drew attention to certain lines and repeated them as being the essence of the thought and feeling being expressed by the poet:

little nameless, unremembered acts
of kindness and of love

and:

when thy mind
shall be a mansion for all lovely forms,
Thy memory be as a dwelling place
For all sweet sounds and harmonies;

She said it was the *moral idea* which the poet was able to show in the poem, it was the essence, the distinction between ordinary speech and poetry and was essential for understanding human life.

The grandmother, unable to sleep, took out the road atlas the three-miles-to-one-inch road maps, to find Tintern Abbey and the River Wye, somewhere above the Abbey, where the waters came *rolling from their mountain springs* unaffected by the tides of the ocean. She began to feel serene, comforted, while she peered through the magnifying glass to discover perhaps the exact place, the steep and lofty cliffs, where the river curves and connects *the landscape with the quiet of the sky.* The place where Wordsworth must have been standing, revisiting, with all the thought and feeling, the moral idea for the poem in his heart and mind and on his lips.

Perhaps, the grandmother thought, there was no need to talk of arrangements for the future straight away. The middle daughter would certainly speak about her expected baby. There was no reason for her to offer explanations, she might explain and she might not. She could expect, in the circumstances, to stay for some weeks. Such a long journey was not made simply for a few days of visiting. She might well have plans to return to London. There was a friend, a special friend, the grandmother remembered from letters in which the middle daughter wrote about the pleasure of being with a woman, because women understood the loneliness of women, and the need for an elevation in their lives, like reading and going to concerts. Sexually, the middle daughter had written, the friendship was perfect. The grandmother had not read Havelock Ellis when she was young but she knew that people discussed orgasm quite openly, though she herself had felt this to be a private subject. Perhaps the pregnancy had disturbed the balance of this affection between the middle daughter and her friend. Perhaps the pregnancy had failed to deepen the affection as hoped. Women brought up babies together now, the grandmother knew this. The grandmother had not known how to reply, in her letter, about the sexual perfection and so left out any reference to it. Because this seemed inadequate she sent a picture postcard of the famous local wildflowers, addressing it to both the middle sister and her friend.

In any case it was clear that the baby would be born soon, with or without explanations. And there was no doubt that the aunt, the eldest sister, in spite of spoken reproach and criticism in long-distance telephone calls from London, often unwanted birthday telephone calls, because the middle sister had forgotten about a birthday present or a card, would straight away hold the new baby somehow, as if in the palms of her large hands. And the lineaments for the new child's distinctive features would be carved in advance, as with the nephews, on these capable hands. Perhaps the new baby, like the nephews, would thrive on the aunt's love. Perhaps the aunt would, as with the nephews, give the child a special place in her thoughts, make the child hers. And, in this way, perhaps the little niece, already present, with her thin arms and legs and her deceitful expression, would receive, as well, the blessing of a rightful share of the aunt's love.

A great deal can happen after a sleepless night. The grandmother, after a lifetime of sleepless nights, knew too that it was possible to feel perfectly well after a troubled and wakeful night, though it was not easy to believe this during the wakefulness. She had discovered that it was possible to carry out, during the following day, all that had to be done. She would start early, she told herself, and she would bake an apple pie.

The horrors of family life, surely family life held

more than simply horrors. An exquisite moment, which came immediately to mind, was the pause when the polished soup spoons hovered above either a smooth potato and leek soup or a chicken broth with pearl barley.

The grandmother quietly pushing a small mop along the floorboards of the hall thought of the pleasure there was in good beams and floorboards, and she allowed herself to dwell on her own good fortune at being able to have a house, of her own, with these good beams and floorboards. She paused and listened at the half-open door of the room where the folding beds were placed side by side, low down on the shabby carpet which, the grandsons told each other, was of pure silk and woven in Persia and was, in fact, a flying carpet.

She heard the grandsons in their early morning conversation, the voices going to and fro like the bird voices in the bushes along the river cliffs.

'Hey, craphead!'

'Hey, idiot, dickhead!'

'That crappy *girl*, man. She's cool.'

'Yeah, cool, real cool.'

'Yeah, cool, that *girl*.'

'There's just a *line*, man.'

'Yeah, cool man, a line.'

'Yeah, craphead, just a *line*.'

'Idiot! You're an idiot. It's a slit.'

The rest of the house, it being Sunday, was silent.

Part Three

Three Times One-Third

II Corinthians, chapter 4, verses 17 and 18

v.17 For our light affliction, which is but for a moment, worketh for us a far more exceeding *and* external weight of glory;

v.18 While we look not at things which are seen, but at the things which are not seen; for the things that are seen *are* temporal; but the things which are not seen *are* eternal.

IT WAS SUNDAY afternoon, the day after the middle sister's arrival. All morning she walked about the house exclaiming about the sun, the blue sky, the fresh air and the coming of the spring at, what was to her, the wrong time of the year for the spring but, all the same, so nice. She did not seem to notice the wagtails, the blue-tailed wrens and the other larger birds, the magpies and the crows and the green parrots, whose intentions for the day seemed to lie in the heart of the blossom where the fruit was beginning to set. The honeysuckle, she declared, was absolutely overpowering, all over the verandah, the way it was, quite gave a girl the headache.

'Travel.' The grandmother suggested that the long journey could have caused the headache. She suggested then that the middle sister should lie down for a rest.

After lunch the aunt insisted that the grandmother should have a rest. And the little granddaughter went to sleep without anyone telling her to lie on the bed.

'If you have the house,' the middle sister, shrouded in a heavy cotton smock and lying on the banana lounge at the edge of the verandah, said to the aunt, 'if you have, I mean, if you *get* the house, I should say, you'll have to pay us each one-third of the current market price. One-third each of the value of the place.'

'That's right,' the youngest sister's husband said, 'this is prime land. This is a paddock left behind in the middle of a high-class residential suburb, practically on the river at that. You'd be living on a gold mine and you'd have to pay for that.' He warmed to his subject. 'If them big trees were to be chopped down, there'd be river views. There's one or two places around here where there's land been left wasted. Fetching good prices, I would say so.'

The youngest sister, who seemed to have no opinions, no voice and no personality since her marriage, did not say anything.

'All this land,' the middle sister sighed. 'It's all far too much for mother,' she said. 'Mother ought to be in a retirement village with bowls and morning teas and games, you know, bingo and square dancing, not to dance herself, of course, just to watch, I mean.'

The eldest sister, the aunt, said that she could not imagine the grandmother enjoying any of that. Bingo was a positive insult, she said, and she could not see how people could think that a person had an educated life in order to end up playing bingo.

'There's a fortune here, right here under our feet,' the middle sister said. 'Once this house is knocked down, there's enough space here for several units and a swimming pool.' The middle sister wanted a sale, she said, and she wanted - *needed* - one-third, a one-third share. Surely they both wanted what she wanted.

The youngest sister's husband understood perfectly. He told the youngest sister, his wife, that she could go ahead, get preggers all over again with a third. 'She's gone broody, really clucky,' he told the other two sisters. 'Since the little girl arrived yesterday,' he said, '*she*, the wife here, wants a girl. A little girl, with pretty eyes and hair.' She's wishing, he told them, for pretty little dresses and dolls and dolls' clothes. 'She never gave me a wink of sleep last night,' he said, 'her going on about a baby girl.' He winked at his wife. The youngest sister smiled and looked down at the verandah boards.

'There'll be one-third each,' the middle sister persisted. She went on to say that she could not see what the problem was. The grandmother drew a pension, didn't she. This place, she said, was far too much work for an old woman. 'Be real!' she said. And then she said that, in her opinion, for what it was worth, old people went on living far too long these days.

'Isn't it time,' the middle sister asked the eldest sister, 'isn't it time you talked to her about death and dying? I mean old people need to be helped to let go. I mean, you can see that she's ready to go. You need to talk, encourage her to understand that the time has come for her to give up, to look forward to dying, everybody's doing it.'

The youngest sister's husband, for once, had nothing to say. He stood up and whistled through his teeth a small tune which had no melody.

'Do you remember?' the middle sister said, changing her voice and speaking quickly as the grandmother stepped out through the kitchen door and on to the verandah. 'Do you remember?' the middle sister asked the aunt, 'do you remember that Christmas, years ago, when you tried to sell your doll?'

'No,' she said to the middle sister. 'I don't.'

The grandmother, looking round and smiling at them all, said that she remembered lots of dolls through the years. She remembered especially the way in which the middle sister, for some reason, had destroyed the other sisters' dolls. Limb from limb, the grandmother told them, she had torn the hair off their heads and, tearing the dolls apart, she had thrown the legs in one direction and the arms in the other direction and, if the eyes could be poked out, she poked them out, or in, whichever way they would go. 'And look now,' the grandmother said, 'here she is with her own little girl complete with arms and legs and hair and eyes.'

The grandmother had felt the aunt's cold hands when she was being made comfortable in the cane chair; she went on talking. She said that she did remember the eldest sister, the aunt, when she was seventeen, selling her doll. She told them that the aunt advertised the doll and all her little frocks and coloured knitted things in the local paper. The price asked was not much for all the loveliness of this doll. She remembered that a woman came and saw the eldest sister and the doll alone in the front room. The grandmother said she guessed that this woman had persuaded the eldest sister to *give* her the doll because there was no money in her purse afterwards. The grandmother remembered too that the front room was decorated with coloured paper chains ready for Christmas and, all the evening, the eldest sister sat quiet and thoughtful, not playing any games or anything, as if she had a dark and lonely space all round her. The grandmother said that when she, the eldest sister, was young she loved her dolls as if they were real babies. She had not wanted to part with her doll but was wanting some money for Christmas for them all, because, at the time, the grandmother was very short for housekeeping.

For the evening meal the grandmother had made a chicken soup with vegetables and pearl barley which the youngest daughter's husband did not really care for, so they left early to go home. Because of the company of the new little cousin from England the grandsons were allowed to sleep over another night, the grandmother having said she would get them both off to school, the next day being Monday. They would walk to school, she said, it being close, and the little girl cousin could walk with them. If wet, the aunt could drop them off on her way to school.

Sometimes early, too early in the morning, when she woke up the grandmother felt anxious. She dreaded old age and death. When she thought about it she understood that it was advanced old age that she dreaded. She was old in any case and there were compensations. People, strangers, spoke in kind voices to an old person, especially she discovered, when she telephoned a shop or the plumber, the young voice at the other end seemed to speak to her with a careful sweetness in response to her old cracked voice. These strangers, in shops or in the street or at the other end of the telephone, they used their first names, Guy or Mark or Jessica or Jasmine, and they greeted her in a familiar way and, if they knew her first name, they used it.

It was when she heard the first tentative bird voices as it was beginning to get light that the grandmother reasoned her way out of the feelings of dread. These soft exchangings of sounds from the birds reminded her of the little voices of the grandsons when they woke in the mornings and began, as if they had never been asleep, to play at once with some game still spread on the floor from the previous evening.

This morning, after hearing by chance an essential part of the conversation from the verandah the day before, it was more difficult to deal with the usual early morning thoughts. She supposed that it was natural for them to expect her to sell her house and land though she had not been able to talk about it with them. It would be a disturbing conversation to have and, as for being talked to death, well she had proved that she could outlive talk, sometimes nearly falling off her chair with boredom. It was the aunt she was concerned about. There had not been an opportunity since the first evening when the aunt (the eldest sister), on the edge of tears, had gone to bed without them, herself and the aunt, coming to a peaceful agreement in connection with the apparent needs of the middle sister and the aunt's own honest good sense.

The aunt stood in the kitchen. She said she did not want to talk about a particularly awkward thing. She was running late for school, she said, but she supposed that the grandmother had not managed to avoid overhearing; 'You will have heard?' she said.

'Yes, I did hear,' the grandmother put her hand on the aunt's sleeve and accompanied her across the verandah to the steps and across the gravel to the car.

'I think,' the aunt said, 'that you must stay here.'

'Of course,' the grandmother patted the sleeve.

'It's what I said,' the aunt paused, 'it's the forerunner.'

The grandmother watched the aunt's little car till it disappeared down the track and round on to the road. She stood for a few minutes, imagining the voice of the auctioneer disposing of the grassy slope of the orchard in convenient subdivisions. She looked at the trees, gnome-like with age, as she was herself, yet every year they yielded the plums, the apricots and the peaches and, from further down the slope, the apples, pears and quinces. A mixed orchard she was told, years ago, was easier to manage, staggered crops her adviser said then. And it was good advice. She made her way slowly back into the house. It was as if she could see already the builders' mess immediately outside her house. There would be the constant ringing of metal trowels on bricks. The builders would bring loud music, dirty greaseproof papers would blow about everywhere and an ugly little building, their portable lavatory, would probably be placed right outside her front door. Whichever way she looked she would see ugliness. And then there would be all the dust . . .

Of course, she understood immediately, she was a stupid old woman, she would not be here and neither would her house be left standing. She looked out, with a kind of shyness, through her kitchen window. The quiet grass sloping upwards and the fruit trees, undisturbed, were very soothing. She could see, in the near distance, the little grandsons, still in their nightshirts, on thin, bent legs crouching, between the trees, searching with diligence through the long grass. They had an empty jam jar each.

'Time to get ready for school,' she called out to them. They were, they called back to her, looking for frogs as a special present for the aunt. It would be a frog circus for her, they said, and it would be all ready for her, in her room, when she came home.

It was later than she realised. Skip school, she thought, the elder grandson could practise his running writing at the kitchen table. And both grandsons, together with the granddaughter, when she woke up, could do spelling and mental arithmetic while she made her apple pie. She reached for the telephone.

'There's a fortune under our feet,' the middle sister's voice sounded still in her head. A fortune wasn't really anything unless it meant that people could have happiness and good health and travel and be together just as the fancy took them. A place meant a great deal and the people coming to the place were the important part of a fortune, good fortune.

The telephone was picked up at the other end and she, at once, gave her explanation.

So sorry I'm late with this letter, I misjudged the length of an orgasm and missed the post. The letter with black felt pen scribbling all over the back of the envelope came from England for the middle sister about ten days after her arrival. The grandmother, as she held the letter, turned it over and over. In her hand it was thick and fairly heavy, but that might simply be because of thick pages. She put the letter on the mantelpiece. The middle sister often slept late, often till midday. The grandmother wondered if she was taking tablets of some sort. The little granddaughter slept heavily and late, but that was from bad habit. She, the child, stayed up far too long at night. Nothing had been explained about the obviously expected baby, and the grandmother did not ask any questions. Though she did ask the youngest sister, who said that there had been no talk between them about anything let alone *that*.

As the days went by more letters came from England for the middle sister. They were always from London and the envelopes, bearing excessive stamps, always had messages written all over them with the same black felt-tip pen. They were illegible messages in initials and half words, often smudged or crossed out. The letters became more frequent, sometimes two arriving with the same post. The middle sister simply took the letters without saying anything about them, not even any kind of exclamation on receiving so many. She never opened or read her letters in front of anyone and she never sat on the verandah or at the table in the house to write any replies. The grandmother thought she would write secretly, during the night, with a cloth over the bedside lamp to avoid disturbing the little girl. But there never was anything to be taken to the post. The grandmother hoped she would not set the house on fire if she was, in fact, shrouding the lamp in an old cardigan or something of the sort.

The grandmother did not ask any questions. Though every morning she, thinking about it, was on the point of asking if the middle sister had baby clothes and nappies in readiness and, if not, should these be bought at once or quickly made at home.

The grandmother had no idea who was sending the letters. She tried to imagine the sender, even though the eldest sister told her to stop being ridiculous and to put her mind to more profitable thoughts. But the grandmother's imagination persisted, even against her wishes. She thought of the letter writer as being a shabbily dressed man, with long hair but almost bald, unhealthy hair tied back with a rag, an unshaven man, pale with hunger, unemployed, a pretend artist or writer. Then again it could be a married man, well off in business, tired of his wife and the respectable suburb, but not prepared to leave her or the suburb or not *able* to leave her because of a family of children which included two sets of twins and a poor little retarded baby, the result of a late pregnancy owing to his thoughtless selfishness. The possible letter writers could make an endless list, a sort of nightmare of people writing letters to the middle sister, even though it was clearly one sender only. Of course the letters might be coming from a woman, a young woman, a girl even, a minx, still in school, but brazen and knowing, holding the middle sister to some terrible ransom, perhaps to do with a sexual crime, something unmentionable and sordid, perhaps even having nothing really to do with the middle sister who might simply be a victim. The grandmother bravely faced the word blackmail.

Minx covered everything from huntress and gold digger to sexpot. Minx, a young woman with a rash on her thighs, ruined hair and a sly expression. Every movement she made displayed a certain vulgarity lacking that innocence, that gift, which some women managed to keep. Others parted with it easily, as if with an inborn internal wish, in childhood. But back to the minx, a predator, a vixen without an excuse since she, at her age, would not be feeding her young.

When stolen chickens were replaced only by the musky unmistakable scent of fox the grandmother, in judgement, excused the fox, the vixen, when it was clear that the nocturnal huntress cough-barking, through the reeds, along the river, was probably lean and mangy, overburdened with hungry cubs.

Or, of course, the letter writer could be an older woman, a divorced woman addicted to drugs and alcohol. Or a widow with strong thighs and wild handwriting which suggested, without specific words, wild desires. At the word orgasm in black felt-tip on the back of an envelope the grandmother experienced a feeling of shock. Mostly this was against herself for imagining the strong thighs of a widow.

There was, as well, the awful thought that perhaps the middle sister was playing minx to an older woman, someone grave and dignified like the aunt who, in the presence of a go-getter (for want of a better word), was helpless and who was begging the middle sister to come back quickly, her devastating loneliness being unendurable. This last was, in the grandsons' word, a crap-headed thought, as a woman like the aunt would never write a message containing certain words on the back of an envelope and send it through the post. It was a good thing that the aunt could not know exactly what the grandmother carried in her head. The grandmother could just envisage the scorn the aunt would heap on her if she did know.

Robbers and cheats, crack addicts and queens in elaborate drag, they played cards for enormous reward or loss; the grandmother, waking suddenly with words, as if from a printed page, in front of her, thought she heard someone calling. She sat up and listened. The aunt, if she knew, would accuse her of reading too many cheap novels and letting her imagination lead her into stupid thoughts. Dreadlocks, in the silence the grandmother remembered an ugliness of hair which, at the time, seemed unnecessary but which the middle sister said was quite definitely a style which was making a statement. It was the kind of hair, the grandmother, sitting uneasily on the edge of her bed, told herself the letter writer, the writer of the sinister-looking letters, would have. Then there were those boots they wore. These dressed up, undressed people wore heavy, lace-up farm boots, the kind which the children of poor people wore when she was a girl. With their expensively shabby cotton denim, these people, they wore these heavy boots. She often saw pictures in magazines. She guessed that their expressions in their eyes, behind the dark-tinted lenses, would show how forlorn they were. The drooping shoulders were in contrast to the calculated appearance of strength in the security of stout boots. Every day she thought about the middle sister and the letters and every day she came to the same realisation that in a family there was always something the matter, always something going wrong, and it was not possible to simply open a door and pass into another room, closing the door softly but firmly on whatever it was that was wrong. Not for the first time during these last days she understood that she was frightened. Fear. She felt cold with this fear.

Never let fear come into your life, someone said to her when she was still a schoolgirl. She had never forgotten this, and here she was, a threatened and frightened woman after being fearless all her life, simply because a daughter, the middle one, without warning and without explanation, had come home seeking sanctuary. When she thought about it, there was no safe place in her house if someone should come, the hunter or the huntress, after the middle sister. Nothing closed properly in the house, the windows were loose in their frames, any keys which still remained would not turn in the locks. She never tried to lock up the house. At night the household was especially vulnerable with three women and three small children and one unborn child sleeping there. She had to understand that she had been afraid for almost four weeks, ever since the arrival of the middle sister. She was afraid to talk openly to the aunt. It was strange to be unable to face confronting and disturbing the aunt. The aunt had straight away, in her usual manner, made her own thoughts and feelings quite clear about the middle sister being there indefinitely. The grandmother could see how reasonable the aunt's attitude was.

The grandmother, at the same time, knew that, as the middle sister's mother, she could not and would not send her away. Where could anyone go in their life if not back, if the need arose, to their own mother, and to that place which was called home with all that a person, having been given life, deserves to have; the safety and the comfort and the love? Who can turn away a son or a daughter? The child is always the child of the mother. Nothing could change this whatever bad or harmful thing that child might do. There was no way in which this thought could be moved from the grandmother's mind. The thought isolated her, she was as if shipwrecked on a desert island, alone with this thought. She was afraid to approach the middle sister, with an ultimatum demanding to know her intentions. She saw always, in her mind, the young mother, alone, and the child's small hands grasping at the mother's skirts endeavouring, on inadequate legs, to keep up with the forgetfulness encompassed in the long striding steps which, in any case, lacked direction. Or if the child was carried, the grandmother slipped from one image to the next, the small arm would reach round the mother's neck, the fingers spread on the shoulder, and the head nestled into the mother's unkempt hair would be nodding with sleep.

Hens, the grandmother said to herself, were better than humans, they did not discard their chickens but went on tirelessly scratching in the dust, pretending to pick up wheat, or delicacies of insect life, so that the chickens, safe from crows under the mother hen's shadow, would imitate this act of pecking. The grandmother lost herself momentarily in thoughts of a particular hen, years ago, who, after hatching some duck eggs, was followed by the ducklings in her shadow. They followed her scratchings in the dust but were not able to peck bits out of the dust. Ducks do not feed that way her father told her then.

A terrible chilling cry sounded through the house. It pulled her from the hen and duckling memories as it must have pulled her earlier, without her realising, from sleep. The cry was followed by another, long drawn out and louder as if the crying had been held back and was no longer being held back. Whatever was causing the cry was too much. Gasping breath and sobs followed and then there was another cry, louder if anything than the previous one. The sounds were hardly human, the grandmother, trembling, fished in the dark for her slippers. She heard the aunt calling that she was coming and the little granddaughter came running, pulling at her nightdress and whimpering.

The grandmother, groaning and singing, it was only childbirth after all, delivered the middle sister. She held and slapped the reluctant baby while the aunt brought warm water and towels to wash the mother and her child. At last the baby cried and the mother, resting, smiled.

Everything comes right in the family, the grandmother told the aunt, when there is a new baby. They rolled the baby in soft pieces of flannelette and made a cradle of sorts in the clothes-basket.

The grandmother turned off the light and drew back the curtains. The moon was high up and the pink fingers of the rising sun were beginning to show at what could be described, on such a night, as the edge of the world. The grandmother told the aunt that she did not like the look of the middle sister. There was too much bleeding, she said. Had the aunt noticed the bottom half of the bed was soaked? They stood in the doorway and looked at the middle sister who was lying very still, as if asleep. She was pale, her face almost transparent in the moonlight.

The grandmother said they must get the middle sister and the baby to the hospital as quickly as possible. She said she thought there was something wrong with the baby as well.

When the aunt said she would drive the middle sister and the baby to the hospital, the grandmother, seeing already the aunt's car failing to take the bend high up on the river-cliff road, said that the aunt must not think of doing anything of the sort. She said that if anything just happened to go wrong the aunt would, for the rest of her life pay for it, blaming herself for ever. She would never learn, the grandmother said, unless she made an effort to understand, that destiny, either her own or someone else's, did not rest with her as an individual. Destiny, a person's life and death, was governed by something beyond mere human power. There was not time to explain or to argue. They must call the doctor to come and he would arrange the ambulance. The aunt must not try to take the middle sister and the baby anywhere.

The grandmother reached for the telephone and gave it to the aunt. And recalling, with some relief, the middle sister's smile, she warmed up some milk for the little granddaughter and put her back to bed.

The grandsons, who were once again sleeping over, slept on undisturbed. The grandmother paused outside their partly open door, listening to them breathing. She thought about these small innocent snorings of childhood and how it was not possible to know what dreams caused children to call out or to laugh in their sleep.

After the doctor and the ambulance had come and gone, with the aunt's help she washed the sheets in tubs of cold salty water. And together they threw the heavy wet things, dripping, over the lines in the orchard to let them blow and bleach out there.

When the middle sister came home from the hospital with the new baby the aunt looked into the cradle and smiled, but made no move to take the new baby into her arms.

The grandsons took turns to nurse their new cousin. Because the younger grandson held his breath, while holding the baby, his face began to go blue. He had to be rescued by his mother, the youngest sister, who, not for the first time, said that she really wished for a little girl with pretty hair and eyes and she wished, as well, she said, for pretty little girl clothes and for dolls' clothes.

In the atmosphere of baby clothes and gentle behaviour the youngest sister said, too, that she was sorry for despising the eldest sister, the aunt, because of her empty purse all those years ago. She had not realised at that time, she said, the emptiness in the eldest sister's heart after she had given away her doll. She had been listening at the door, she confessed, that evening and had heard the woman, who looked like a gypsy, tell the eldest sister that *she* had everything and the little sick girl, who was lame, had *nothing*, no nice clothes, no toys and no doll. And yes, she said, the boys could sleep over if it wouldn't be too much for their grandmother.

The grandmother, later, washed the grandsons' hair surreptitiously, the aunt having said firmly that they were getting old enough to wash themselves.

A long pony tail, unwashed, earrings amazingly

ugly in loops and matching the ugly loops of the gold chain round the neck, the middle sister wore gold and silver bangles on both arms, several of each. She was hampered by this jewellery she declared, and was not able really to handle her baby. She lay back on the sofa as if helpless.

'Can't she get up and get her own cup of coffee?' the aunt, unable to hide the impatience in her voice, said.

'It's having someone bring a cup to you that's important,' the grandmother explained. 'It's important to be waited on sometimes.'

The jewellery flashed and rattled and *weighed a ton*; the middle sister found something to complain about every few minutes.

'As if she needs to wear all that,' the aunt again voiced an opinion. 'Surely there's no need to wear so much decoration *here*.'

Faced with a mother and a newly born baby, the grandmother said that they must accept both the mother and her baby. She wondered uneasily where the middle sister's ornaments came from.

'It's all fake in any case,' the aunt said, 'it's not an expensive gift from anyone.' She was sure of that.

The grandmother felt better at these words from the aunt and saddened, at the same time, because it seemed clear that no one had given a present to the middle sister after all. It was difficult to know which was the least troublesome of the two alternatives, the idea of the middle sister being compromised with gifts and obviously unhappy, or unhappy in any case and having to comfort herself with such stupid and vulgar decorations purchased for herself by herself. The grandmother thought too that the middle sister should have a nice haircut and a shampoo in a shop. This would be a small contribution towards a detail of real cleanliness and would, at the same time, be a little bit of pampering during a condition which seemed frightening in its similarity to a severe depression. Something which women seemed to suffer from more often in the present times.

The middle sister refusing, as soon as she left the hospital, to feed her baby, complained all the time that she was in pain and that her discomfort was intolerable. She screamed about this. The grandmother, unable to persuade her to nurse the child, put fresh cabbage leaves on the swollen breasts and pinned a folded tablecloth firmly round the leaves to keep them in place. The younger sister also failed to persuade the middle sister to feed her baby. She was obliged to help the grandmother with the bandaging. They did this while the aunt was at her school. The grandmother made the decision that the baby would be bottle-fed. 'The milk must not be encouraged in the breast,' she said, tightening the tablecloth.

The middle sister complained about the noise the

grandsons and her own little girl made. She could not stand, she said, the repeated bouncing of a ball on the verandah boards. This was something the grandmother had not even noticed. She wished the middle sister's voice was not so disagreeable. This voice had a depressing effect on the household.

The middle sister refused her food. She did not want to eat, she said. And she did not want to look at the new baby girl, even when the youngest sister, bringing left-over gowns and little jackets, spread them on the middle sister's quilt so that she could make a choice.

The grandsons and the little girl cousin were sent to play in the far corner of the orchard, as far away as possible from the middle sister. But noise persisted. There was the endless clatter of dishes and a child, running into the house and out of the house, would let the fly-screen doors bang both times. Repeatedly.

The grandmother considered the characteristics of her daughters. If the eldest sister, the aunt, could sit waiting out the whole day, waiting for the whole day to pass as on her birthday, which she did not want to celebrate, the middle sister had even more determination. It was as if, in her unhappiness, she was staying on in the house, as if by simply being there she could squeeze them all out of the house and off the land. The grandmother could not, of course, mention the thought to anyone but there seemed to be a possibility that the middle sister was creating an unhappiness from which there could be no escape, unless the property was sold and everyone given a share so that, in the middle sister's way of thinking, they could all be happy with the money and follow their own ways and be free of one another. The grandmother was not sure how much of the middle sister's behaviour was because she was really ill or whether something from her way of living had infected her and this, perhaps, being a shameful illness, was being kept secret. She did not want the middle sister to bear this alone and, at the same time, she felt she could not invade her daughter's privacy. There was the thought too that her daughter was being hounded for money. The grandmother had always been subject to ambivalence and, silently, she cursed herself for this weakness in her own character.

The grandmother wished for the friend the middle sister had written about, at one time, with such apparent contentment. She wished that a letter would come from this friend. The letters with the curious messages scribbled with the black felt pen on the backs of the envelopes could not come from this friend, who understood the need for concerts and reading and going to the theatre, *the elevation of life*, the middle sister had written in her own letters.

This friend, the grandmother indulged in some thought, this friend she would be wearing now in November, in London, a nice warm tweed, a straight skirt with discreet box pleats, front and back, pleats, from the knee, a cream blouse, quite plain, and a tailored jacket fitting perfectly on the shoulders. The wool check would be in small squares, light and dark brown like the Harris tweed. Her low-heeled shoes and heavy stockings would be of good quality and she would have a soft leather handbag, brown with a shoulder strap, not shabby but not new either. Her short hair would be parted on one side and touched very lightly with grey and she would have a kind expression in her eyes. She would be both gentle and wise and her voice low and musical, contralto if she sang . . . The grandmother knew she was, in her thoughts, giving the middle sister the aunt as her friend. Did the friend (the grandmother dismissed the aunt), did the friend want the middle sister's children to bring up as her own little family or was the whole trouble because the friend did not want children at all; or, was there some man involved who either wanted the children or did not want them? And was the trouble even more complicated by addiction to some drug which required more and more money? The middle sister was not a child. No one at the hospital would discuss her health with the grandmother. If there was some secret trouble the grandmother did not know how to reach into it.

The eldest sister, the aunt, and the youngest sister helped the middle sister in all sorts of ways but they did not have sympathy for her. The aunt said plainly that sympathy only made the middle sister worse. 'She complains the whole time,' the aunt said as calmly as she could. She said that the house was no longer a place to come home to. She went off for a walk by herself. The youngest sister came with the grandsons and some more baby clothes and little pillow cases. When she heard that the aunt had gone out she said she could not stay and, even though it was the weekend, she took the grandsons home with her, straight back home without the grandmother even being able to give them a biscuit each. The grandmother watched them being bundled, long faced, into the youngest sister's car. She watched the car go down the track and turn, out of sight, into the road and a sense of desolation came over her. She stood in the sweet scent of the honeysuckle, sad and alone.

The orchard trees were pretty still with blossom and the fruit, the Satsuma plums, the prune plums, the nectarines and the peaches had begun to set, tiny green nipples, scarcely visible, but which the birds would feed upon.

The grandmother stood in the bleached grass, the sun hot on her back. Slowly she set to work, putting plastic bags on to the branches which she could reach. She chose the thin branches which would take clothes pegs. This way, when the bags blew and rustled, and remained attached, the birds might be kept away from some of the fruit. While she worked there was no sound from the house, no complaining voice calling. And the baby was not wailing. For a time the grandmother was forgetful of everything except the fruit trees and the fading blossom. She worked but, at the same time, she was resting in the silence and the peacefulness of her orchard.

The little granddaughter came, picking her way through the long grass. She told the grandmother that the new baby was going to have a bath and she was going to have a bath as well. Her mother had said so.

'Is mother going to have a bath too?' the grandmother, brushing flies away from the child's face, asked.

'Yes,' the child told the grandmother. 'All, her and me and baby.' The grandmother was surprised. This was a surprise, as the middle sister had been refusing to wash even her face. And, of course, the baby and the granddaughter had been bathed. The grandmother was wondering what could have produced this change.

The bath was full of hot water. The grandmother said that it was too full and too hot. She said that the baby should be bathed in the little zinc tub in the kitchen sink, and, in any case, one bath a day was enough for the baby. The grandmother was out of breath from hurrying down from the top of the orchard slope. The little granddaughter was pulling off her clothes.

'No,' the grandmother said. She steadied herself on the door post. 'Give me the baby,' she said to the middle sister who was standing in her night-dress in the small bathroom. The baby was naked, the thin little body was rigid under the middle sister's arm. It was hot with steam in the small space. The grandmother felt faint. The middle sister was indistinguishable. The grandmother knew she was not seeing her properly. 'Give me that baby,' she said once more.

If you have imagination, a teacher said once to a room full of girls, if you have imagination, you can go all round the world, if you want to, on a luggage label on a suitcase belonging to a perfect stranger. And, in the same way, it was possible to step into a different layer of society on the merest breath of passing cigar smoke. The grandmother wondered why, at this particular moment, she remembered this.

The middle sister, in a movement of defiance, held the naked baby, its extended arms and kicking legs small and helpless, over the hot water.

'Take your dress,' the grandmother said to the

little granddaughter, 'and go out on the front verandah and watch out for auntie coming home.'

It was right to honour and acknowledge the stories in the mythology simply because of their existence, but no one would really believe that Ceres could produce from the red-hot embers a robust, laughing and contented child to replace the puny prince she was nursing. Unless, of course, the grandmother saw reason at once, the meaning within the action was a metaphor for trust. That was it. Imagination and trust.

'You must trust me,' the grandmother said in an even, quiet voice, 'when I say this water is too hot, you must believe me.' In spite of herself, her voice trembled.

The middle sister let the small body slide under her arm. The grandmother, weak, in the emptiness of the afternoon, heard her own ineffectual voice and, as she looked at her middle daugher she saw, with some shock, that it was possible for the child, the grown-up daughter, to hate the mother. She wanted to ask the middle daughter not to look at her in that hard way. She wanted to take and hold the baby and to feel the soft smooth skin. She wanted to gather all the agitated movement into her own arms. She wanted to bury her face in the baby's small nakedness. And she wanted to speak out to the middle sister. She wanted to tell her that there was only one way and that way was to take and accept all that which happens in your life and simply to push on with living in the face of accusation, misunderstanding or whatever it is with whatever subsequent unhappiness. A person is never unhappy for ever she wanted to explain, and every person has some unhappiness or grief to bear.

'Give me your baby to hold,' her voice, groaning and cracking, pleaded. 'Let me hold your baby,' she crooned, moving on to words of comfort. She wanted to tell the middle sister that she could not be threatened because it did not matter what was said about her to her own mother. The grandmother thought of blackmail. 'You must trust me,' she said, trying to make some music in her voice, which kept disappearing in a croak and finally a cough.

The baby seemed to be slipping. The middle sister held the tiny body pinned to her side with her arm and, because of this, the grandmother noticed, the child was not able to breathe properly. The stranglehold, reminiscent of a headlock, gave the grandmother courage. The middle sister was not letting the baby fall.

'Come along then.' Her lullaby of entreaty continued with a few words emerging now and then.

The middle sister was leaning towards the grandmother.

'Imagine,' the grandmother said, indicating the bath with a movement of her head. 'Try and picture this,' she said. The grandmother wanted to speak about remorse and how this feeling could be more powerful than greed or jealousy or revenge. She was afraid of using the wrong words. She was afraid of making the middle sister more unreasonable. She wished for the right words. 'Only try and imagine . . .' she said.

The baby was slipping. The middle sister, leaning more towards the grandmother, swayed in the narrow space. The baby began to slip from the slack arm. The grandmother, trembling, reached with both hands.

'You know,' the grandmother said to the aunt, 'your nickname, which has persisted, came from her. When she began to talk she couldn't pronounce your name.' She told the aunt that the middle sister, with her lisp and late speech, named the youngest sister as well. The aunt said that she remembered.

They sat together, the grandmother and the aunt, in the rose purple of the sunrise watching a bank of dark cloud dispersing. The grandmother, having predicted rain, withdrew her prediction. Her cane chair, the shabby but acceptable furniture for a verandah, creaked as she leaned forward to pour tea from a battered teapot. She was shrouded in an assortment of shawls, layers of knitting and crochet in a variety of bright colours, caught in front, pinned together with a large ornamental pin belonging to generations of hoarded clothes. The November evenings, the nights and the early mornings were wind-swept and cold, a striking contrast to the heat, which built up during the days as they unfolded towards the full summer.

As the night of sitting and waiting for the aunt's return had spread into the long hours of the whole night, the grandmother, rummaging, found more shawls and rugs and draped them on her shoulders and knees. She had plenty of time, she found, during this night to think about a number of things, one of these being the middle sister's special friend, the one the grandmother imagined as a widow with strong thighs and the wild handwriting suggesting wild desires. This whole idea, once again, surprised the grandmother, but mostly this was because of thinking about the friend in this way for, of course, wasn't she a widow herself. During the night the imagined picture of this friend had changed. She told the aunt she would explain everything. She had, she said, envisaged the aunt sitting out the night on the flat rock on the river cliff, watching the changing colours of the water till there were no colours, only the light which comes from water as it is the last thing to get dark. The grandmother did not mention anything about the aunt being capable of endurance, of sitting something out, her unwanted birthdays for one thing.

The aunt tried to tell the grandmother that she was sorry she had not come back from her walk. She knew she should have been there to help the grandmother. She was sorry, she said. The grandmother interrupted the aunt, she wanted the aunt to know that small children, relatives, old people - even cripples on sticks and crutches and walking frames together with paralytics in wheelchairs - are a sort of protection to a house. They make a kind of barricade when something of the sort is needed. Did the aunt understand this, she wanted to know. These people, the grandmother said, the very things which are a hindrance, are a protection simply because of their needs. They defy intrusion. They prevent change. Or, by being absent, bring about change.

'I had the house and the middle sister and her children to myself last night,' the grandmother said. During the night, she explained, she doubted her own fear because she could not quite believe in it. She asked herself whether the performance put on by the sisters was intentional. Were the sisters trying to force her to sell her land or to force some sort of catastrophe in order to bring about a dramatic change? Finally she came to a conclusion. She thought not. The behaviour was simply family behaviour, when people in the family do not know what to do next. There was no plan of any sort. Simply a mother and three sisters floundering. During her life, she explained, she had often floundered. Hopelessly. She was sure the aunt must have noticed.

'When I look at both the little girl and the baby,' the grandmother said, 'I don't see any family likeness in either of them. The baby is a replica of Queen Victoria.'

The aunt reminded the grandmother that she always said this about newly born babies. And, since none of the sisters had ever seen a portrait or even a postcard of this queen, the comparison had no meaning. She supposed it was the pursed mouth and the little chin, receding, and the way in which new babies, before they learned to smile, often looked as if they disapproved - when they weren't bawling their heads off.

'Not the grandsons,' the grandmother said, 'I never said this about them.'

The aunt reminded her that the grandsons were atavistic. They were really more like monkeys, she said. She said that for a time she had had serious misgivings about their cranial space.

The aunt, unrelaxed once more, again said she was sorry that she stayed out all night.

'It was the best thing you could have done,' the grandmother said. 'We had a grand hair cutting,' she indicated with a jerk of her head the middle sister's bedroom window at the far end of the verandah. 'A nice hot bath and a hair washing. And what's more she tore off those cabbage leaves and fed the baby.' The grandmother paused. 'It was a bit like having her here as a little girl again,' she said. 'I don't think she would have done any of this in company. I mean the bath, the hair and feeding her baby. She had to climb down. She never was one to climb down. She was always the proud one. The dancer. Remember?'

Pudding basin? The aunt remembered the hair cuts of childhood.

No, the grandmother told the aunt, I took that terrible long pony tail and I cut it, it was the Mozart first and I kept on cutting and it's the urchin now. She gave a small laugh. They had quite a night of it, she told the aunt. 'Picture this,' she said, 'we even called, long distance, the friend in London, not the black felt-tip, but the *real* friend. Remember? This friend apparently has the Dance Group. She's a dancer too.' The grandmother gathered from the overheard half of the telephone conversation that there had been a row because of the baby, but that was all over now. The quarrel was made up, she said, just now on the phone. 'Just a few words and some tears at both ends. Just like a film it was. That was all that was needed. After that she went to bed.' The grandmother nodded once more in the direction of the middle sister's window. 'Not a squeak,' she said, 'from her or the baby, since.'

The grandmother supposed that the middle sister would stay for Christmas and then return to London. 'And the children?' the aunt wanted to know. A mother and her children should not be separated, the grandmother told the aunt, 'unless there is some specific reason.' The grandmother was adamant, she said.

'Everyone has to pay for something during their lives and I don't mean money,' the grandmother said. 'This comes from a long way back.' She could never understand, she told the aunt, how that King Pelias could allow his three daughters to boil him in a cauldron to bring back his youth to him; whether the special herbs were included or not, as far as the grandmother was concerned, she said, the pain must have been intolerable. Even if not believed, the myth had to be acknowledged, for did not all myths attempt some kind of explanation for those things which remained forever a mystery. The grandmother knew that she must show her scalded foot and leg to the aunt.

Yes, she told the aunt, she had to step in the bath. It was the only way to reach because, as the aunt would know, the space where they were standing in the bathroom was too narrow.

Yes, she said to the aunt, she agreed she must see the doctor straight away. The pain, she said. She had some home treatment, there was cold tea in the pot. What more could she have done?

They would have to go to the hospital, the aunt said, it being Sunday. And at once.

The grandmother did not argue. Indoors, in the grandmother's room, where she shed a number of shawls, the first sunlight dappled and, flickering in the restless green foliage outside the window, filtered through the lace curtains giving the room a secretive serenity as if it was under deep water.

The grandsons arranged their cereals in order of preference on the verandah table and gave the little girl cousin what they felt was a fair share of the milk.

The grandmother sat at the edge of the verandah with her foot, bandaged heavily, on a cushion. In her lap she had a chipped enamel bowl from which, with her claw-like hands, she scattered mean servings of grain. The hens had discovered with incredible speed that food was not being brought to them. They had made their way, with industrious peckings, up to the house. The grandmother hoped that her thoughts would remain invisible. She wished it could be possible to leap right over Christmas and into the hoped-for tranquillity beyond.

'Oh this heat! It's unbearable and it's not even half-past seven.' The middle sister batted her eyelids at the youngest sister's husband. She sat with her skirts drawn up so that her thighs were uncovered. The heat was terrible, she said. 'Get me a glass of iced water,' her voice purred in his direction.

The grandmother, though the son-in-law was the opposite of all she had ever hoped for, knew that a flirtation with him would be impossible. The youngest daughter would never be in danger of losing him. She thought this was a pity and then corrected herself immediately because wasn't he the father of the two grandsons? There was such a thing as gratitude, she admonished herself. He had his uses; it would never occur to him not to go to his work, that in itself was a blessing. The son-in-law fetched the glass of water and gave it to the middle sister with hardly a glance at her.

Inside the house the baby was crying and the aunt was making tea. The grandmother heard the kettle boiling and wished that she did not have a bandaged foot. Unaccustomed to illness she disliked being incapacitated in any way. She tried to take pleasure in the spectacular flowering of the purple creeper which grew right over the shed at the top of the orchard. She was impatient with her disability. Her impatience even spoiled the cup of tea which the youngest sister placed beside her. Her bandaged foot cushioned against the boards no longer ached and throbbed with pain. She did not know whether this was a good sign or a bad one. Supposing, just supposing the foot, or part of it, fell away in the bandage when it was taken off. She knew such things could happen. She remembered an eye and part of a man's face in the blood-stained gauze of a removed dressing when she was nursing years ago . . .

It was easy to be frightened once you had let fear into your life. Fear repeated her visits, unexpectedly and always unwelcome. She glanced sideways at the middle sister and wished that she was more motherly. She wished, for example, that she would pick up her crying child now, right now. She wondered whether the friend, the partner, would have patience. She thought of the two children, the small girl and the baby, left for hours alone in the damp room which, she pictured, awaited the middle sister's return. She could see, in her thought, this semi-basement room in a tall London house in a long London street. The floor covering in this room would be a thin carpet, cast off from some other house and too big. It would ride up the damp wall on one side of the room . . . Her thought was interrupted by the middle sister who had moved to sit on the verandah steps with her hairbrush and hand mirror. Would they all just look at her hair. She could not do one thing with her hair. Would they, she insisted, just look at the mess which was her hair. The middle sister kept on.

The baby had stopped crying. It was most likely that the aunt, instead of drinking her tea in peace, had picked up the fretful little creature. This family breakfast had been the grandmother's own idea. She did not want the aunt to bear the entire burden of it. She told the elder grandson to fetch the baby, she would do the nursing, it was just about all she was good for.

The verandah. The grandmother, taking the baby to replace the enamel bowl on her lap, thought about the verandah. It was the place where that little art which is family life is practised, where great battles take place and the linings of the garment, which is the human body, are exposed but even then, the soul, if such a word can be used, is not completely revealed. It was strange, the grandmother reflected, how people hid themselves even in families where they should not need to hide. The verandah, she reminded herself, was a place for overhearing and it could be the place for reconciliation. The middle sister, she noticed, was still wasting her energy on the youngest sister's husband. He would never see anything of this. Fortunately he was such a fool.

Of course, the middle sister probably did not live in a damp basement in London. The grandmother thought it would be wiser to try and curb her imagination and her anxiety. The number of runaway trucks which had mown down her daughters during the years of their childhoods exceeded all possible countings. Having the baby, even a discontented baby, in her lap comforted her. She would nurse and cherish this child into some kind of happiness before the time crept up to and over Christmas. She looked at the middle sister who was still angry with her own hair, beating it with the small hairbrush, frowning at herself in the hand mirror and saying that they ought to have a swimming pool in a terrible climate like this. She could not wait, she told them, to get back to England. Thank heaven, she said, she had made the booking for her return flight.

The grandmother, crooning, did not stop rocking the baby. She looked across at the middle sister and longed for the airport lounge and that special time, those wonderful few minutes of peace, when people were slowly leaving to go home after the plane had taken off.

'My hair!' the middle sister said.

There was a pleasant fragrance of bacon coming from the kitchen where the grandsons were helping the aunt and their mother, the youngest sister.

'My Goddam Hair!' The middle sister wanted them to see all the impossibilities.

The grandmother, putting the baby up to her shoulder and feeling the softness of the baby's cheek against her own, remarked that there was really only one week between a bad haircut and a good haircut.

OTHER BOOKS BY ELIZABETH JOLLEY

The Well

One night Miss Hester Harper and Katherine are driving home from a celebration, a party at a hotel in town, when, in the deadly still countryside, they knock something down. It's a man, whose body they proceed to dump, with great difficulty, in a farmyard well. The next morning cries are heard coming from the bottom of the well . . . An extraordinary, original novel with Elizabeth Jolley's usual potent mixture of scarcely suppressed violence and eroticism.

PENGUIN – THE BEST AUSTRALIAN READING

OTHER BOOKS BY ELIZABETH JOLLEY

My Father's Moon

The story of Vera, as schoolgirl, student nurse and unmarried mother. It is a story of naivety and love, and above all, of survival in England during the grim years of World War II. It is moving, evocative and laced with the wry humour which characterises Jolley's work, with a very deep, grim undercurrent.

PENGUIN – THE BEST AUSTRALIAN READING

OTHER BOOKS BY ELIZABETH JOLLEY

Cabin Fever

Vera has cabin fever. Confined with her thoughts in the concrete tower of a New York hotel, she is haunted by her mother's reminders of what she should have been, and the desperate choices she faced as an unprotected single mother.

PENGUIN – THE BEST AUSTRALIAN READING

OTHER BOOKS BY ELIZABETH JOLLEY

The Georges' Wife

'*Once I told Mr George that I was afraid he would leave me or that he would not want me any more and he, nursing me on his arm, told me that most people ultimately have the experience of having only the memory of love . . .*'

Vera and Mr George have made a new life together but Vera's thoughts return again and again to loves and lovers, meetings and partings, the voices that echo in the mind like music.

What has she learned from the well-bred peace of the Georges' household; the decadence and disorder of her friendship with Nöel and Felicity; the fun and vulgarity shared with her 'widow' on the long voyage to Australia? Must we always repeat the past?

As in *My Father's Moon* and *Cabin Fever* Elizabeth Jolley returns to the themes of discord and harmony between brothers and sisters, husbands and wives, friends and lovers. Her spare and sensitive prose is illuminated with compassion and understanding for the intricacies of human relationships.